SINS IN BLUE

A NOVEL

BRIAN KAUFMAN

Black Rose Writing | Texas

©2020 by Brian Kaufman
All rights reserved. No part of this book may be reproduced, stored in a retrieval system or transmitted in any form or by any means without the prior written permission of the publishers, except by a reviewer who may quote brief passages in a review to be printed in a newspaper, magazine or journal.

The author grants the final approval for this literary material.

First printing

This is a work of fiction. Names, characters, businesses, places, events, and incidents are either the products of the author's imagination or used in a fictitious manner. Any resemblance to actual persons, living or dead, or actual events is purely coincidental.

ISBN: 978-1-68433-479-7
PUBLISHED BY BLACK ROSE WRITING
www.blackrosewriting.com

Printed in the United States of America
Suggested Retail Price (SRP) $16.95

Sins in Blue is printed in Chaparral Pro

*As a planet-friendly publisher, Black Rose Writing does its best to eliminate unnecessary waste to reduce paper usage and energy costs, while never compromising the reading experience. As a result, the final word count vs. page count may not meet common expectations.

To my friend, Brian Gasser

SINS IN BLUE

CHAPTER ONE: THE COPPER STILL

"You like ribs? /
My daddy took a bat to mine."
~Willie Johnson, *Misery Train*

1969
Pittsburgh, Pennsylvania
Kennedy Barnes chose a barstool away from the window, but halfway into his first beer, the evening sun angled his way, leaving him blind. The sun's rays lit his pilsner glass, gold on gold. The rest of the bar was dark. He removed his John Lennon frames with the Coke-bottle lenses and rubbed his eyes with his palms, careful with the right eye, which was black and sore. *Wonder what Mom would say if she saw me now?* he thought. He reached into his jacket pocket for the tenth time to be sure the small tape reel was there. Everything else he owned sat in a duffel bag at the foot of the barstool. A few shirts, underwear, a toothbrush, and three hundred dollars rolled and wrapped in a rubber band. No record collection—that was in shards, scattered across his bedroom floor back home.

A pang of despair hit him. His record collection had been everything. Then he remembered the tape in his pocket. *Almost everything. I have two songs left, and they're my ticket to the big time.* He downed his beer in one long swallow and glanced around the room, looking for a clock. When the bartender passed by, crisp in his black-and-whites, Kennedy asked, "Do you have the time?"

"Six o'clock. Another Black Label?"

"Thanks, Mabel."

The bartender frowned. "First time I've heard that one . . . today."

Kennedy winced. "Sorry about that." He slid his stool to the left while the bartender poured him a second beer. "I've got a bus to catch at six-thirty."

"Here you go. Should I tab you out?"

"You probably should. I can't miss that bus."

The bartender turned to his register and grabbed a ticket. "Where are you headed?"

"Fort Collins, Colorado."

"Never heard of it."

Kennedy wrapped his hand around the beer glass and pulled it closer. "Small town north of Denver."

"Business or pleasure?"

"Business." The bartender seemed suddenly attentive. The bar was nearly empty. Perhaps he wanted a tip.

"What's your line?"

Kennedy tapped his glasses frame twice with an index finger. "I'm in the music business."

The bartender raised an eyebrow. "Cowboy music, is it?"

Kennedy snorted in his beer. "Oh, no. Hell no." He grabbed a bar napkin and wiped his face. "No, nothing like it."

"You a musician?"

"Nope. I'm a manager."

"Really?" The bartender slid the ticket across the mahogany bar top and tilted his head, a thin-lipped smile on his face. "Do you represent anyone I've heard of?"

"You heard of Chuck Berry?"

"*You* represent Chuck Berry?"

"No, of course not. But a lot of people think Chuck Berry invented rock and roll. Some say Ike Turner did. Either him or Arthur Crudup."

"Who is that?"

"You probably don't know him. He wrote *That's All Right* and *Rock Me Mama*."

"So, you represent this Arthur guy?"

"No, no." Frustration crept into Kennedy's voice. Talking to the bartender was like talking to his father. "The point is, Berry and Crudup are supposed to have invented rock and roll. But they didn't. Not by a long shot." He paused to take another sip of beer, more for dramatic effect than thirst. Instead of waiting for the punch line, the bartender turned and walked to the other end of the bar, where the only other patron nursed an empty rocks glass.

The sun's light angled again, coming to rest in Kennedy's eyes. He fished a bill out of his duffel bag and set it on top the bar tab. Time to go. *My future is waiting.*

"Hell of a shiner you got going there." The bartender stood with a linen napkin in hand. He grabbed a wine glass from the overhead rack and began polishing. The glass looked clean, but the bartender stood in the shadows, so who could tell?

"Yeah. I've been known to speak out of turn."

"How's the other guy look?"

He shook his head, thinking of his father. The thin taste of lager turned sour on his tongue. *I could still go back home. Mom would let me in.* By tomorrow, the locks would be changed. Too late for apologies, then.

"So, what were you saying? Something about the invention of rock and roll?"

Kennedy burped. "Excuse me." He wiped his mouth on his sleeve. "My client invented rock and roll in the thirties, during the Great Depression."

The bartender pursed his lips. "Wow. What's his name?"

Kennedy laughed. "Sorry, can't divulge that. Not until I get him under contract."

"Ahhh," he said as if he'd solved a great mystery. He grabbed the bar tab and the cash. "Change for you?"

"No, keep it," Kennedy said. He'd wanted change—needed the change—but the words just slipped out. "You're not making much money today, are you?"

The bartender chuckled. "This is a businessman's bar. My regulars come in after seven. Speaking of the time, it's ten after six, my friend. Not chasing you out, but you might want to get to the station early."

"I would." Kennedy took a last glance around the bar. "Wish I had a little more time, though. I'm getting hungry. Do you do to-go orders?"

"They serve steaks and chops here. Takes a while to cook." He paused. "Let me poke my head in the kitchen and see if I can whip something up." He passed by the other customer, whispered something, and headed for the back of the bar.

Kennedy stepped off his stool, frowning. Had the bartender guessed he was underage? What kind of trouble would he be in if the police came? His father would *never* come bail him out. Drinking in a bar? Wasn't he proving they were right about *everything*? "Christ on a crutch," he muttered. "I do *not* need to go to jail."

The bartender came back carrying a packet wrapped in aluminum foil. "Here," he said, holding it out. "It's a sandwich. I was going to eat this on my break, but they can make me another." Kennedy reached for the sandwich and stopped, wondering if the food was bait and the bartender would grab his wrist and restrain him. The bartender stuck the sandwich in his hand and walked away, shaking his head.

"How much do I owe you?"

"Nothing, nothing. It's just a sandwich." He glanced back over his shoulder. "You take care, okay?"

Kennedy nodded and turned to go.

"Hey, kid?" The bartender pointed at the duffel bag. "You're forgetting your bag."

Too embarrassed to say more, Kennedy rushed over, grabbed the bag, and headed for the door. Halfway to the bus station, he glanced down at the sandwich in his hand. *Damn, I'm hungry!* Tipping big had paid off. Or maybe the bartender just felt sorry for him.

After all, not every adult was an asshole.

• • • • •

As the bus rolled across an empty stretch, the road winding like a ribbon around a desolate package of dirt and scrub, he leaned against the window and tried to sleep. The noise coming from the seat behind him made that impossible.

A woman tried to calm the baby in her arms, cooing and shushing between kisses. A young boy in the seat next to her had no luck sleeping either. "Mom, he won't shut up!"

"He's hot and he's tired. He'll calm down if you stay calm. I need you to settle down—"

"I'm not the one who's clabbering!"

"Donny, please!"

The baby wailed louder.

Kennedy stood, pretending to stretch. He wanted a glimpse of the drama unfolding behind him. The mother's stringy blond hair was pulled to the side and tied with a rubber band. Her thick shoulders cradled the screaming infant. The boy next to her couldn't have been more than five or six. Bowl haircut and tears.

A woman across the aisle scowled and shifted in her seat. *That will help, lady.* Kennedy shook his head just as the woman with the baby looked up, her eyes black with rings. She met his gaze and then looked down at her baby. *No, no, I'm not frowning at you—I'm frowning at that old bat next to you.* He waited a moment, hoping the woman would look up so he could smile. She ignored him, so he sat back down.

"Mom—"

"Donny! I can't do this. You have to be quiet!"

"But he's getting on my nerds—"

"Donny!" She hissed the boy's name, and then the boy began to scream.

"Mom! You're hurting me! Ow!"

Kennedy winced. *Should I offer to help?*

"Excuse me," the woman across the aisle said. Her voice was a nail on aluminum siding. "I must ask you to attend to your children—"

"Are you blind?" the blond woman asked. "I'm trying to get two children to their grandparents while their father is halfway around the world fighting for your freedom, by the way, instead of helping *me* with our—" Her voice broke off in tears of rage.

Kennedy turned, peering over the top of his seat. "Ma'am? Can I help?"

"No!" she snapped.

"Sorry. I just thought that your son"—he kept his voice low and pointed to the older of the two boys— "might come up here with me. I have an open seat, and I'll watch him for you. You look like you could use a hand."

The woman stared, her mouth open.

A man sitting directly behind the woman stood, a grimace on his face and a three-day stubble on his chin. "Hey, kid? Leave the lady alone. She's got her hands full. She doesn't need your guff."

"I was trying to—"

"*This* is why we shouldn't go by bus!" The woman on the other side of the aisle shoved her husband's shoulder. He gazed straight ahead without answering.

The man with the stubble pointed. "I told you to sit."

Kennedy turned and sat.

"What's going on back there?" the driver called.

"We're fine . . . now." Stubble man to the rescue.

Kennedy lay his head against the window, eyes closed and his hands clenched in his lap. *I ought to beat that guy's ass.* He considered the other man's size and decided he couldn't afford to be kicked off the bus in the middle of nowhere for fighting.

Behind him, the baby stopped fussing, but Donny continued to weep, a single low moan like the root note of a chord. The melancholy sound reminded Kennedy of his brother. Jackson was only six. He wouldn't understand why Kennedy was gone. Family arguments always frightened the little guy. *No more arguments, now that I'm out of there.* The thought made him sad. His father would say what he wanted about Kennedy, and his mother would be silent—the same as agreeing. Jackson would grow up believing Kennedy was weak and worthless because that's what they'd tell him.

Kennedy sniffled. The bus smelled bad. Too many people packed close together. The dank odor of wet upholstery made him sick. Sometime after midnight, when the driver made a gas stop, he bought himself a fruit pie and a Coke, but the pie tasted stale and he only ate half.

. . . . .

1969
Fort Collins, Colorado
Willie Johnson stacked the supply cart full of bath towels, hand towels, washcloths, and sheets. He slipped a few bottles of general-purpose soap into the corner, making sure it didn't tip. The cart was a big canvas basket on wheels with no shelves. He had to watch for spills. One bottle with a loose cap had tipped over a year earlier, and Mrs. C had bitched about it for three months. Loaded with clean linens, he pushed the cart into the hall.

Steering was a problem since the cart had no handles. He gripped the sides and bulled his way up the motel hallway, stopping every ten paces to catch his breath. First stop, Bella Dickerson, the crankiest maid in the motel.

"Well, by God," she said when he arrived. "Ah been waiting for half the morning for some clean sheets. You been off somewhere sleepin'?" Bella's voice carried a raw kind of southern drawl, too full of cigarettes and cotton burr to sound like home.

"No, ma'am," he said. "There ain't no rest for the wicked."

Bella snorted and grabbed a stack of bath towels from the cart.

"Slow down, Bella. You took half the towels I got, and there's other girls working that have waited just as long as you."

"Slow down yourself, old man. On second thought, don't do that. The only way to be slower is to stop dead." She brayed at her joke, throwing her head back.

"I ain't gonna argue with you," Willie said, refilling Bella's soap dispenser. "The weather has me down. Hotter than hell out there. Has me melting into my shoes."

"Fill that soap all the way to the top."

"I do every time."

"Only because I remind you every time."

Bella had been a maid at the motel for twenty years. She claimed she'd once been a dancer, but Willie didn't believe it. The woman was stocky as a pug, and she'd have been rough on the eyes even if she'd kept all her teeth.

"Thought you had a trainee today. Somebody to help your sorry old bones."

Willie shook his head. "Didn't show."

"What's wrong with young people these days?" Bella asked. She took one of Willie's fresh washcloths, wiped her face, refolded the cloth, and put it back with the others. "I can't imagine why they're hiring young kids here. Kids nowadays don't know nothing about work. Besides, there's people who need jobs to feed their *babies*."

"Don't I know it."

Bella groaned, one hand to her hip.

"You all right, Miss Bella?"

"No, I ain't all right. And don't you *Miss Bella* me."

Willie began loading Bella's dirty laundry into the canvas cart, shoving the wet things into one corner. Bella was Willie's least favorite maid. She complained about him to Mrs. C at least once a week. For that reason, he kept her stocked, and when possible, he took a moment to chat with her. Truth was, he hated the sight of her pasty white face. At lunch, the crew sat in the break room together, so he couldn't help but see what everyone ate. Bella packed a lunch fit for three people. Onion and cheese sandwiches, peanut butter and mayonnaise. Half a round of Schloss, still in the rind. A bag of Corn Diggers and the inevitable piece of fruit, because *I got to eat healthy, y'all*. Most days, the sights and smells in the lunchroom left him unable to eat.

"Well, Bella, I got to get moving. I'll be by later with more linen."

"Too much later, and my rooms will be all done. I can't milk the clock like you laundry boys do."

"Well, if I *do* milk the clock, I'll save you a quart."

She waved him off with a frown and stepped back inside the room to clean. Willie gripped his cart and pushed ahead. Lenore sang at the end of the hall, and when he got close enough, he could recognize the tune. "Say," he called. "That's a nice old song."

Lenore had blocked the room door with her maid's cart. When she came to the door, he could only see her from the neck up—she was the shortest person on the staff. Her round, smiling face peered over the lip of her cart. "Bringing in the sheets, bringing in the sheets," she sang.

"I thought the word was *sheep*."

Lenore laughed. "I know what the words are, Willie Johnson. But if I'm going to sing the Lord's songs, I'm going to shape them to fit my day. That's how *He* would want it." The open side of her cart faced into the room, so Willie had to pass her linens over the top. She nudged the black frames of her eyeglasses and said, "See? I'm bringing in the sheets." She gave him another laugh and started singing again.

"Yes ma'am," he said. Lenore was dotty as hell, but she had a good heart. He liked her pink cheeks and her white hair. He liked to imagine her as an actress. She'd have been the perfect Mrs. Claus in a Christmas play. That, or the murderess who baked arsenic cookies and killed all of her neighbors.

"I'm headed on now, Miss Lenore."

"I'll see you later, Willie. Don't work too hard."

"No chance of that, ma'am."

He pushed ahead until his breath gave out. Resting with his eyes closed, he listened to the music of the building. The fan at the end of the hall had a ping. Fluorescent lights buzzed overhead. His pulse throbbed in his temples, setting the rhythm. *Ninety beats per minute. Slow blues, something in a minor key. Not a minor 7th. That's too pretty for this place.*

Looking up, he spotted a young man at the end of the hall, hands in his pockets, wearing a Chevrolet trucker cap. Mustard stains dotted the belly of his white tee shirt. "You Willie?" he asked.

Willie nodded. "You Rodney?"

"Yup."

"You're late."

"Don't worry about it."

Willie stopped to breathe again. With the wet things, the cart was heavier than when he started. "They only give you one day's training here. And you're getting a half-day."

"I said, don't worry about it. I'm a quick learner. And this ain't rocket science, is it, old man?"

Willie frowned. *Another smart-ass. Young kids know everything these days.* "Well, come on, Mr. Quick Learner, we got work to do." The boy didn't offer to help as Willie pushed past him. Instead, he followed at a distance, humming to himself. Willie waved him on. "When you have enough laundry to hand out to the girls, you send it up the dumbwaiter and load it into this cart." He stopped to point back down the hall. "The linen station is back that way."

"See? That was easy, wasn't it?"

"Didn't mention cleaning the linen yet. The shoemaker's elves aren't doing the laundry. You are."

"Little soap, little water. Is that still the recipe?"

Willie nodded.

"Then we're cookin'."

Willie stopped in front of Jessica's cart. She was the last of the upstairs maids to be serviced. Jessica was a good-looking girl just out of high school, and when Rodney saw her, his voice changed from a cocky drawl to a good imitation of sincerity. "Hi there! My name's Rodney. I'll be doing Willie's job here in the future."

"Are you going somewhere, Willie?" She pushed a strand of blond hair out of her eyes and tilted her head.

"Not going anywhere, Darlin'. Rodney is training."

Jessica smiled in apparent relief. "Good. You could use a hand, couldn't you Willie?"

"Nice to know there's someone my age working here," Rodney said, leaning closer. "At least there's someone I can talk to."

Jessica stared at him for a moment, smiled, and turned away without saying anything else. Rodney watched her walk, nodding to himself. "That girl has a fine ass."

Willie circled to the other side of his cart and pushed his way back up the hall. "Come on," he said. "I'll show you the linen station, and then I'll show you the machines downstairs."

"Machines is machines." The drawl had returned.

"Yes, they are, which means they're picky. You have to treat them just right to get them to work like you want."

When Willie paused again, puffing and leaning on the cart, Rodney reached in and took over, shoving the cart ahead. "Let me get this, old-timer."

"Old-timer, my ass," Willie said.

"How old are you, anyway? Probably don't want to say, so let me ask you this—what was Abe Lincoln like?"

Willie trudged after him. "He was better lookin' than you, for one thing."

Rodney looked back over his shoulder, smirking. "You're a funny old guy. I kind of like you."

Willie tried to keep up. The boy walked fast. "So, what do you do in your free time, Rodney?"

"I'm a musician. Got me a band—a power trio, like Cream. This job's just to tide me over. I'll get a record contract someday, and I won't look back. I already know what kind of car I'm gonna buy."

"You play music?"

"A Thunderbird Landau. 429 cubic inches of V8. Big-ass car like that, I'll take up two parking spaces wherever I go and fuck 'em, you know what I mean?"

"What kind of music do you play?"

"Rock and roll. We're a power trio. Weren't you listening?" He stopped in the middle of the hallway, letting go of the cart. "You probably don't know what that is, right? A power trio? It's a guitar, bass—"

"And drum," Willie said. "I know what it is."

A smile spread across Rodney's face. "Say, that's cool. You like music?"

Willie nodded. "I played some, back in the day."

"Let me guess. Church music? Gospel?"

"I played some of that," Willie said. "Played some of everything, truth be told."

"You still play?"

"I do."

"What kind of guitar you have? I have a Fender Mustang. I'm going to get a Flying V as soon as I get a few paychecks here, though. The Mustang is just a sled. Soon as I get a better guitar and amp, I'm gonna sound like Clapton." He closed his eyes and leaned back, his hands moving as if he had an invisible guitar. He stopped and popped open one eye. "You play electric?"

Willie stepped forward and began pushing the cart again. "Nope. Got an old flat top acoustic."

Rodney strolled alongside, his hands back in his pockets. "So, did you play in a band, or just solo?"

"Both."

"You make any money at it?"

"Yes, I sure did. Made my fortune. I just work here because I like motels."

Rodney stopped walking and Willie kept on. "You're playing with me, right?"

Willie shook his head.

Rodney caught up at a trot. "Seriously, did you play a lot?"

"For about ten years.'

"Why'd you give it up?" Curiosity aroused, the boy's drawl had disappeared again.

"War came."

"Civil War?"

Willie scowled. "Let's make a deal. You quit with the old jokes, and I won't ask if you need your diaper changed, okay?"

Rodney laughed. "Fair enough." They'd reached the linen room. Willie opened the door with the key he kept hooked to his belt loop and reached in to flick on the light. The opening to the dumbwaiter was inside, to the right. The rear of the room and walls to the left featured floor-to-ceiling shelves, all empty. "When the motel has a lot of linens, we store extras on these shelves. Right now, money's tight, so we're delivering as soon as we wash and dry." He pointed to the laundry chute behind the door. "We dump our dirty linen here and pick it up downstairs."

"There's no chairs up here," Rodney said.

Willie shook his head. "No time for rest." He glanced at his watch. "Lunch in a half hour. Did you bring something?"

Rodney shook his head. "I was running late and left it on the counter. Too bad. I packed two sandwiches and some chips."

"I can share my lunch with you."

"Nah. There's a restaurant across the way. Guess I'll buy my lunch." He walked to the dumbwaiter. "This goes to the laundry?"

Willie nodded.

"I could just about fit in here, couldn't I? You ought to give me a ride—"

"Quit foolin' around. Mrs. C would have my hide if I broke that thing. Besides, I don't want to haul towels and sheets up those stairs. It's hard enough walking up and down with empty hands."

"Who the hell is Mrs. C?"

"Your boss," Willie said.

"I thought her name was Simpson."

"It is." Willie began feeding dirty linen into the chute. "Come on now. Help me with this. I'm off work tomorrow, and you're going to have to do all of this on your own. I don't want to hear anything about how I didn't train you right."

"If her name is Simpson, why do you call her Mrs. C? What does the C stand for?"

Willie stopped moving linen. He stared at his hands, wrapped around a dirty sheet. He tried not to sound angry, but he was tired and he didn't like this kid. "You're a smart musician fella. What starts with C? You'll figure it out."

CHAPTER TWO: THE TOWN PUMP

*"Young people have forgotten to cry the blues.
Now they talk and get lawyers and things."*
~Big Bill Broonzy

1969
Fort Collins, Colorado
When the bus stopped in Fort Collins, Kennedy approached the ticket counter to price fares to Newport, Rhode Island. The ticket agent, a chubby woman old enough to be his aunt or his grandmother, consulted a fare chart and gave him the bad news.

"That's a lot." Kennedy glanced down at his duffel bag. The festival in Newport wouldn't happen for another four weeks. He needed to buy two tickets and have enough money left over to live for a month, plus pay for food on the road. "I'll be buying two tickets. Is there a price break when you buy two?"

The woman glanced over the rim of her glasses. "No," she said, ending with a snort like he'd asked the stupidest question ever uttered. "Are you purchasing tickets now?"

"No, I was just checking prices."

She hummed and tapped the fare card. "Prices subject to change."

"Maybe they'll go down."

She snorted.

He grabbed his duffel bag and wandered up the street, staring at the shop fronts with their sun-faded awnings and dusty window glass. The sun was bright, hot, and dry. When he reached the corner, he looked west and stopped. Mountains, speckled with white, rose up from the flat horizon as if they'd thrust straight up out of the ground. Had it snowed recently? The weather was hotter than hell. How could there still be snow on top the mountains?

He stood still, his duffel bag in hand. If he'd seen a more beautiful sight, he couldn't recall where. *I should call Mom.* The thought came from nowhere, and it made him grimace. For better or worse, he'd arrived in Fort Collins—1,400 miles from home. *I'll do what I have to do.*

Dizziness overtook him for a moment. The bag pulled at his wrist as if he were carrying bricks. He passed a café and a drugstore and then crossed the street to a small pub called The Town Pump, which sounded promising. He could pump a beer or two down his throat and figure out his next step.

The Colorado sun glared like a spotlight. *I need sunglasses.* He stopped, his hand on the door. *No. You're not buying anything but the necessities.* He wiped his mouth with his sleeve. Beer would taste good.

The Town Pump seemed dark and familiar—just like home. Pittsburgh was perpetually fogged with iron and coke from the smelters. His father called the brown cloud the "haze of commerce." Once inside the bar, Kennedy let the cool air swallow him. All the place needed was a Steelers game on the television.

He took a seat at a table in the rear, leaning back against the bare brick wall. Neon signs over the bar advertised "Coors." When a waitress approached, he pointed at the neon and said, "I've never heard of Coors. Is that a beer?"

"Sure is."

Dark or not inside the bar, he could see the waitress well enough. Slender hips, blond hair cut in a bob, and a cute, lopsided sort of smile. "Well, I usually drink Schlitz, but I'll try a Coors."

"Sounds good. You have an I.D.?"

He struggled to keep his expression blank. "Really? I almost never get carded."

She shrugged. "It's a college town. We card *everybody*."

"Damn," he said. "It's hardly worth it. I guess I'll have a Coke."

She narrowed her gaze and smiled. "Coke it is, then."

By the time she returned with his drink, he sat in full pout—shoulders slumped, a downcast expression, and a darting gaze. "I brought you a root beer," she said. "The Coke comes out of a gun, and it's always flat." She set an open bottle on the table. "Costs the same, but this tastes a whole lot better."

He looked up.

"I drink root beer," she added. "I like your glasses, by the way."

"Thanks."

"Do you like the Beatles?"

"I like all kinds of music," he said. "That's actually my business. I'm a manager."

"Really? Any acts I'd recognize?"

"No, not unless you like the blues." He took a sip of his root beer. "Say, this is pretty good. Not real beer, of course, but it's good for root. Root beer, I mean."

She laughed. "You're funny." She glanced around the bar. "We're slow today, but I have to keep busy. The boss is behind the bar. I'll be back in a few minutes. Can I get you anything else in the meantime?"

"No," he said. "Wait. Is there a pay phone nearby?"

She pointed to the rear of the bar. "In the hall back there. Right next to the men's room. Do you need any change?"

"Yes. I'm going to be making a long-distance call."

She stood still for a moment, waiting, and then stepped back. "Well, I can get that change for you any time."

He nodded. "Thanks."

Once she left, he checked his pocket. Two quarters. *I should have given her a couple bills.* He tapped the tabletop with his index finger. *I'll bet that's why she waited around. Idiot.*

He grabbed a five-dollar bill from his bag. When she returned, he pushed the bill at her. "If you get me two dollars in quarters, the rest is yours," he said.

"Thanks." She smiled, her lips raised on the right, tugging at a dimple. She looked adorable.

"I'm calling back east. I'm booking an act for the Newport Folk Festival."

"Will two dollars get you enough quarters?"

He considered the question. "You might be right. I could end up on hold. Better give me another dollar's worth."

She nodded and headed for the bar.

Two new customers—college guys, judging by their clothing—came through the front door, accompanied by a blinding burst of sunlight. The waitress shielded her eyes for a moment, and then squealed a hello, running forward to hug them each in turn. The door closed behind them, returning the bar to the shadows.

Well, that's not cool. Kennedy took another sip of his root beer.

When she returned with his coins, he thanked her without further comment and went in search of the pay phone. He knew the number by heart, having called several times already. At the operator's cue, he fed the machine with quarters and waited for the call to go through.

"Mr. Wein's office. How may I help you?"

"Kennedy Barnes, calling for George Wein."

Silence. Then, "I'm sorry. Mr. Wein is out of the office. Would you like to leave a number?"

"I've left my number before. Besides, I'm on the road. Any number I give you will expire before I get a call back." He paused. "When will *George* be available?"

The first time he'd called Wein, Kennedy had given his home number without thinking. He secretly feared that Wein had returned his call, only to speak to his father. Afterward, he resolved to keep calling until Wein came to the phone in person.

"I'm sorry, but I don't know when Mr. Wein will return. Can I take a message?"

"I've left messages."

"I'm sorry—"

"Okay. Tell me this—did Mr. Wein receive the tape I sent him?"

"Tape?"

"I sent a tape reel. A copy of a copy, but it was Phillips tape. Good quality—"

"I'm sorry, sir. I don't open Mr. Wein's mail."

Kennedy bumped his head against the pay phone once, twice. "Okay, okay. Can I ask a favor?" Without waiting, he plunged ahead. "Ask Mr. Wein—George—to look for the tape I sent. It came in a brown mailer. The return address was Pittsburgh—"

The operator interrupted, asking for more money. Kennedy gave silent thanks for his waitress and fed the pay phone the last of his quarters. "Are you there?"

"Yes sir, I'm still here."

"Please try to find the tape and make sure he listens to it—"

"I'm sorry, sir, but Mr. Wein tends his own mail."

Kennedy groaned. Time was running out. "Please, please, can you write down a message?"

"Of course. Go ahead."

"Tell Mr. Wein that rock and roll wasn't invented in the fifties. It was invented in the 1930s by an old bluesman named Willie Johnson. The tape I sent you came from one of Rickman's aluminum disk recordings. You can hear the file number at the start of the song and everything. The tape proves rock started way before anyone thinks. And I have the original rock and roller under contract. Mr. Wein needs to get him on stage in Newport for the—"

The operator interrupted again, but he was out of quarters. Kennedy slammed the receiver back in the cradle and punched the wall. How could he book his act if he couldn't connect with Wein? How many quarters was it going to take?

He walked back to his seat, deep in thought. Wein should have received the tape a week ago. Kennedy acquired the recording through a friend of a friend. He'd been corresponding with other record collectors, extolling the greats, sharing thoughts on how to build a collection without breaking the bank, and arguing the kind of minutiae that fired the imagination of blues fanatics. Through those connections, he began writing to Patricia Hawke.

Patricia ("not *Patty*—Patty is a *girl's* name") worked as an intern at the Library of Congress in Washington. She claimed to be cataloging the Alan Lomax recordings, something he initially distrusted out of hand, much as he'd questioned the photo she'd sent. No woman *that* beautiful would write a Pittsburgh kid to argue how Lomax's preference for prison music over church music influenced popular perceptions of the black community. "Lomax liked sinful music," she wrote. Staring at the picture she'd sent, Kennedy decided he liked his music sinful, too.

The Holy Grail of all blues collections was housed in Washington at the Library of Congress. Alan Lomax was a musician and scholar. He traveled the back roads of the country in the Twenties and Thirties, making field recordings of authentic American music, including the blues artists that speckled the heavens of Kennedy's pantheon. Using an RCA disc-cutter that etched the sound directly on aluminum discs, Lomax and his father recorded the likes of Lead Belly and others.

Patricia wrote Kennedy often, talking about her adventurous life cataloging music. He replied to her letters with lies of his own (assuming she wasn't being strictly truthful).

Then the tape arrived with a terse message, and everything changed.

Dear Kennedy,
The world has turned upside down, and you are the only one I can share this with.
We received a letter from someone named Willie Johnson. He claimed to have recorded for Mr. Lomax and wondered how to get a copy of the recording. He was fuzzy on details, owing to having been "drunk off my ass" when he recorded the songs. He is living in Colorado, of all places. I was curious, so I searched the discs, which was no small feat. As I've mentioned, there are tens of thousands of discs to sort through.
Well, I found his two songs. One was a slow blues without much to recommend it. His singing voice was a little froggy. But the other song!
I've enclosed a tape. I suppose I've broken every rule possible by sending this to you. Willie Johnson should be playing at Newport and recording for Columbia. If you negotiate a deal, I hope you'll remember to include a finder's fee in the contract!
The enclosed song was recorded in 1934. The name of the song is "Bitch Train." (How drunk was he?) There's no mistaking the shuffle rhythm and

the beat. And the guitar work? You won't believe how many notes someone can jam into twelve bars.

She concluded with Willie's return address and her signature closing, "With all warmth—Patricia." Kennedy immediately pulled out the tape player his mother had given him for Christmas. The recording quality was bad (and the copy he'd sent Wein was even worse), but he could make out the song well enough. The guitarist punctured the chug-chug rhythm with bursts of high-speed blues runs, like Clapton on amphetamines. He listened to the two-minute song again and again while the sun played a light requiem on his bedroom wall. By the time it was dark, he knew what his future held.

If only Wein would play ball.

And Willie, of course. Willie's letter proved he was still interested in music (and was still alive). Kennedy needed two things. He needed a signature on the contract he'd copied from the library, and he needed Wein to answer the damned phone.

Kennedy sat with his back against the brick wall, looking around the room. The pretty waitress was busy talking to her two friends. Too bad—if she knew how close he was to being famous, she'd have paid him more attention. He closed his eyes. The sunshine and uncertainty outside could wait while he made his plans.

Once Willie signed, Kennedy would negotiate a record contract. He'd have to hold some sort of auction among the various record executives and take the highest bid. As soon as he got his share of the money, he would fly home and confront his father. *Here you go,* he'd say. *Take Mom out to dinner and a movie. Pay the mortgage ahead a little while you're at it. It's on me. You know, the son who'll never amount to anything, listening to nigger music? Well, guess what?* He finished his root beer and smiled.

· · · · ·

After work, Willie walked home, cutting across the Colorado State University campus. His feet hurt all of the time, so he moved with a loping sort of gait. Bella, the maid, said he walked like an ape, which made him angry and self-conscious. On campus, though, he was invisible. Young people attending the summer semester moved past him like a river flowing around a bridge pylon.

The bright sun felt good on the back of his neck. The laundry room at the motel was humid like New Orleans—the kind of heat that suffocated a man. On campus, the sun's dry warmth danced with the thin breeze to the sound of rustling leaves and the laughter of pretty young girls. Walking home took him an hour—the happiest part of his day.

Crossing through the plaza by the student center, he ran into a crowd, gathered to listen to a political speech. When Nixon sent troops into Cambodia, the campus became a cauldron of heated opinions. Two overweight boys in dress shirts waved a flag at the periphery. The rest of the crowd looked like the remnants of a sleepover—sweat suits, mismatched tee shirts and shorts, and enough hair to give a barber a wet dream.

"We have to decide! We have to decide what we're going to do!" The speaker's megaphone cut through the rumble of voices. "We can do this like they want us to, all calm and polite, and hope someone listens. Or we can tear this place down! But one thing's for sure. Whatever we decide, we have to stick to it! We're in this together! And we'll do whatever we decide, together. Because we're all in this together! Am I right?"

Some of the crowd shouted back, clapping and cheering. Others stood silent, arms folded.

With his head turned, Willie caught his foot on a seam in the concrete, nearly tripping. *Watch your step, old man.* He looked around. The eyes of bystanders were on the man with the megaphone, not on him. Willie walked on, his limp more pronounced. His hip would never be right, and it altered his gait. The knee took the brunt of it. *Bursitis. Better ice that when I get home.*

Glancing back, he looked at the second-floor balcony of the student center, overlooking the student plaza. Students lined the railing. Conspicuous by his nondescript dress, a man in a plain suit watched with arms folded. Willie stopped to look closer. The man wore no expression. Plainclothes detective or FBI? "Hello, Captain," Willie whispered.

Below the rail, half the crowd stood and the other half sat. Megaphone man shouted again. "*Those against using any means?*" The students who had been sitting stood up, while others sat. "*All right then, that was pretty close, but for now, it looks like—*"

"Excuse me!" A boy stepped back, hands in front of him as if to ward off an attack. He wore a brown and tan tie-dyed jeans jacket and glasses with black plastic rims.

"Sorry there, fella," Willie said. "I should watch where I'm going."

"That's okay. Sorry about that." The boy sidestepped, yielding the right-of-way.

Willie gave a slight bow and moved on. From behind, megaphone man chatted up the crowd, trying to draw cheers.

Politics. *A waste of time.* Unless the government was headed by Hitler or Stalin, killing their own damned citizens, the things politicians argued over didn't amount to much. Decades of staying in and out of trouble taught him a few simple rules. Stay away from the police or end up in a crowbar hotel. Hands off another man's muffin. Don't bump your gums. Mind your business and other people will mind theirs.

Anything else was a trip for biscuits.

Past the library, the crowd thinned out, and he could breathe. He liked seeing so many young people, and he longed for some kind of contact, but crowds agitated him. That didn't strike him as a contradiction. In his experience, people were generally nice as long as they didn't congregate. Paired up, they turned into something else. Something dangerous, if enough of them got together.

He stopped to rest, sitting on the benches outside the liberal arts building. A young girl at the other end of the bench smiled and he smiled back.

"Hello. How are you today?" She was shouting. Perhaps she thought him deaf.

"It's a beautiful day," he answered. "The sun feels good on my face."

She tilted her head back, her freckles and red hair tinged with the sun's rays. "You're right," she said. "I'm glad you said so. You reminded me to notice."

She reached into her backpack, rummaging through the contents. "Do you live here in town?" she asked without looking up.

"Other side of campus."

She glanced at him, a shy smile on her face, and asked, "Do you belong to a church?"

Oh, damn. "No. Had a church back home."

"Where's home?"

"Mississippi."

"I'd never have guessed! You sound—"

"Been all over," he explained.

"Well!" She pulled a pamphlet from the backpack and scooted across the bench. "I belong to Mercy Farm."

"The pie people?"

She laughed. "We do make pies, the best in town. That's how we fund our outreach missions. We're a church—"

"I know," he said, a cold sort of finality in his voice.

"Well," she continued, seemingly oblivious, "I thought that if you'd like to find a place to worship, you might share our fellowship."

He stood up, clutching the pamphlet. "I'll give this a look when I get home," he said. "So nice to talk with you."

She beamed. "So nice to talk to you!"

He walked on, chewing on the things he hadn't said. Wasn't Mercy Farm more of a commune than a church? They funded their efforts by demanding that new members donate everything they owned to the group. The girl, though, was a cute young thing. Pert little breasts. He had suppressed an urge to say *I'd like to try a slice of your pie*. That sort of thing could get him killed, of course.

"No, Sugar," he said. "No church. I've been dancing in the Devil's fire far too long." Too bad—he'd wanted to talk to someone. *Anyone outside of work*. And she'd been friendly enough, church talk aside.

The subject of religion called to mind the Washing the Disciple's Feet Resurrection Ministries back in Mississippi. Those people would have burned Willie at the stake if they'd had their way. Some of the congregation used to stand outside the juke joints and shout "sinner" at him, and he'd always laughed at them. The idea of sin struck him as funnier back then.

Almost home. Willie lived in a small white frame house west of campus. The place was older than he was, with just one bedroom, but the rent was cheap. The landlord didn't like renting to students, who tended to tear up a property. For years, Willie had done minor repairs on the place for free, which endeared him to the owner, though lately, he had no energy left over for pipes and rafters. The summer before had been hot, and Willie hadn't done a good job with the lawn. Big patches of brown bracketed the front walk. One of the two shrubs beneath the front window had died. Someday, maybe soon, the old bastard would take a long look at the lawn and raise the rent or evict him, and Willie would be on the street. If Willie were younger, he might rent a place with two or three students and split the rent, then stick the savings straight into the bank. As it was, he had $311.75 in his savings account (a penny or two more if the bank had posted interest) to show for a lifetime of sweat and excess.

Music is no way to get rich.

He paused inside the front door. The postman had dropped two advertisements through the slot. The letter he wanted wasn't there.

When leaving for work, he'd vowed to clean up the front room. Another broken promise. Gathering up the dirty laundry meant taking everything to the laundry mat, and he didn't have the energy. He grabbed a pizza box off the couch and jammed it into the trash can next to the refrigerator, pushing down until the box fit. The dirty dishes could wait, too.

He hobbled over to the bedroom and sorted through the books stacked inside. Tonight, he'd grab something light like Burroughs. Old Edgar Rice could spin a tale. The problem involved finding the right damned book among the stacks, some of them waist-high. He found most of his reading material at used bookstores, though a fair number of the volumes were stolen from the college library. The piles had grown taller over the years.

Sifting through the stacks, he found Robert Howard's boxing stories. Willie didn't like Conan, but he loved the boxing stories, all of which centered on heroes who could take a punch. Willie could take a punch. He had to. Over the years, he'd lost most of the fights he'd been in.

He restacked the books and took his Robert Howard into the front room. The sun still shone and would for a few hours. No need to fix dinner. His stomach was being finicky again. Later, he would eat a few Rolaids and get some sleep. For now, he would slip into a book.

The hero, Mike Brennan, had a "granite jaw and a chilled steel body." And no defense. He took a hammering, fight after fight, trying to make enough money to marry sweet Marjory, who would always love him, win or lose. The story made him smile. By the time Iron Mike Costigan finally knocked poor Brennan out, ending his fight career, the Fort Collins sun was setting.

Willie set the book aside and stared across the room. His beat-up Kalamazoo sat propped against the record shelf, whispering to him. The pull of music was inevitable. He walked into the kitchen, filled a small glass with whiskey, and carried it into the front room. Grabbing the acoustic guitar, he sat down on the couch, took a sip from the glass, and began to play.

He warmed up with Big Bill Broonzy's *Key to the Highway*. Eight-bar blues, simple as pie, but he fumbled the seventh chord on the turn and stopped. His fingers felt old and stiff. He played a simple blues run in A. *Sounds like a kid at a lesson. Shit.* He stretched his fingers, shook his hand, and ran up and down the scales until his fingers warmed a little. Then he started the song again.

He played on, running through old favorites. He didn't play any of his own songs, but that was merely a postponement. He would have to play the *one* song. Sometimes, he went a week without playing it, but tonight, as the room faded to dark, he would return to *Sins in Blue*.

The last of the light slipped away, washing the color from the couch and curtains, draping him in gray. He began to play, picking his way through the melancholy melody. His playing was not perfect, but now the mistakes—owing much to his poor, old fingers—sounded real and true. Like so many nights before, the song made him weep.

When he finished, he leaned the guitar back against the record rack. Then he fetched the battered pillow and blanket from the end of the couch and settled down for another long night. He might sleep. Tomorrow was a day off. Not having to worry about getting up early sometimes helped.

Eyes closed, he thought about the song and the things he'd done, which left him swallowing the acid at the back of his throat. He'd forgotten the Rolaids, but he was too tired to fetch them from the bathroom. He shifted on his back, trying to take pressure off his hip. His knee ached—he'd forgotten the ice pack, too. He tried to think of something else. He always came back to music. He remembered the first time he played a juke joint, and that made him smile, which in turn let him settle into the couch and rest a bit.

CHAPTER THREE: THE SPINNING MULE

"Saturday night is your big night.
Everybody used to fry up fish and have one hell of a time.
Find me playing till sunrise for 50 cents and a sandwich.
And be glad of it."
~Muddy Waters

1927

Cruger, Mississippi

Willie Johnson sat alone in the corner of the room on a three-leg stool, his arms draped around his guitar. The sun was still up and the air was hotter inside the juke joint than it was outside. Sweat crawled down his back, soaking his dress shirt. He wore pressed trousers and a tie, but the tie point showed—he couldn't afford a jacket, nor would he wear one in this heat. His shoes had three miles of mud on them.

The crowd wore their best—something they could worship in, come morning. They would dance all night and head straight to church without a pause. He wondered how they'd stand each other's smell in the pews.

The juke stank like mildew and shine and cigarettes. Willie took a sip from his glass and set it on the floor. *One, that's all. There's already enough blind bluesmen.* Moonshine distillers made their hooch by re-distilling industrial-grade alcohol. Not to let an opportunity go by to kill their citizens, the government had changed the formula for industrial alcohol, adding methyl alcohol to discourage bootleggers from re-distilling stolen industrial product. Nobody warned anybody, Willie decided, because people ended up blind or dead, which seemed to please the politicians. If it kept up long enough, poison hooch would result in a sober America.

Willie had seen the effects of a bad batch firsthand. Three drinks each, and a half dozen men and women went blind. Two dancers ended up as dead as if they'd danced on a rope. After that, he limited himself to a single drink a night, unless he knew the distiller.

His friend was out on the floor with that girl again, putting the spin in the Spinning Mule. Jackwash was his usual smooth self, whirling and hoofing without a drop of sweat on his face. He'd slicked his hair into place with enough Murray's Pomade to lubricate a truck. With that and his pencil mustache, even Willie had to admit Jackwash cut a fine figure. The girl sure thought so. She twirled on cue, but her eyes were locked on Jackwash the rest of the time. Her mouth had a puffy sort of pout that was half-smile and half-hunger.

She *should* be hungry. Bony thing had no cushion.

When the song ended, Jackwash looked to the band—an old guitarist and a drummer—and nodded in Willie's direction. The guitarist shook his head, holding up one hand. *No, not yet.* Willie slumped on his stool. *How long am I going to have to wait? These people aren't taking me serious.*

Jackwash came over, grinning like everything was going as planned. "You'll get your chance," he said. "Quit worrying. Damn, by the look on your face, somebody just died."

"I'm just anxious to play."

Jackwash held onto the girl with one hand and pointed with the other. "See that fella over there? You know who that is, don't ya'?"

Willie nodded. "Sure do. Man's a damned legend." He'd been watching the bluesman all night.

Jackwash leaned in closer. "Well, if *he* likes you, that'll be worth the wait." He glanced back at the girl, and then down at his hand, as if he'd just noticed the two of them were attached. He pulled her forward. "This here's Luella."

"We met before," Willie said.

She tilted her head to the side, as if to regard him. "No, I don't believe so."

Willie snorted. "Watch me play. You'll remember me, then."

She gave him a pretty little smirk. "Your friend is mighty sure of himself, Jackson."

Jackwash gave her his best wide smile, the kind that melted girls like Luella. She melted all right, though that was easy enough to do inside the juke. "Willie and I go way back. *All* the way back." He turned to Willie. "Luella's gonna sing tonight. She got a fine voice."

"Maybe I'll stick around and listen," Willie said. "Right now, I gotta think about playing."

"Let's leave this man alone with his guitar," Jackwash said, stepping away. Willie could barely hear him. Another song had ended, and the dancers were making a ruckus. Willie waved at his friend and stared at the floor.

Jackwash—Jackson Washington—had been his best friend since childhood. They played ball together, fished, and even stole fruit pies from the church window. When Willie got caught, Jackwash faded into the tall grass. The reverend had Willie scrape old paint from the walls inside the church for a week's worth of evenings while Jackwash sat on the riverbank eating pie. That was the story of their friendship.

One evening, while filling a Mason jar with fireflies, Willie decided to say something about his friend's name. Willie's daddy had been drunk early, and cuffed him a few times, so Willie was in an ornery mood. "You know your name ain't real, don't you?" he said.

Nine-year-old Jackwash stopped running around and stared at him, a perplexed look on his face. "Course it's real. It's a real name."

"A real name's when you get your uncle's name or your granddaddy's name. Somethin' to do with family." He looked up from his firefly lantern and smiled. "You named for two presidents. Andrew Jackson and George Washington. It's kind of a joke if you think about it."

Jackwash stood there squinting, and then his face opened up into a smile. "What about you?"

"What about me?"

"You got two dick names. Willie and Johnson."

Willie sat down, dumbfounded. The thought had never occurred to him. Sensing it was no time to give in, he doubled down. "I'm calling you Jackwash from now on. Don't be surprised if everyone calls you that for the rest of your days."

Jackwash shrugged. "Willie," he said. "Johnson."

Nothing had changed. They were contentious friends, forever bound, forever bickering. Jackwash was better at everything else, but he couldn't play the guitar. When it came to music, Willie had it all over him. Part of that was on Jackwash—the boy couldn't sit still long enough to practice. When Willie got good enough to play here and there without embarrassing himself, Jackwash conceded that particular competition. "You the musician, all right. I'm glad. There's gotta be *one* thing you're better'n me at."

Playing jukes was part of Willie's long-term plan. He'd go on the road, traveling from town to town, playing for meals and pocket money. *Should be easy. I play this thing like I have eight fingers on each hand.* But to get his foot in the door, he needed Jackwash. Jackwash knew the folks who ran the juke. He ran shine for them, and cleaned up the place after the sun came up. And Jackwash knew the gnarled legend in the corner of the building—sitting with his eyes closed, bobbing his head to the rhythm of the song. In some ways, knowing people was more important than knowing how to play.

A roar of laughter behind him made him turn. The back room was stuffed full of men gambling—both cards and dice. Between illegal liquor, gambling, and food, the juke owner made a good living. Outside, where women cooked, the smell of fish and hoppin' john—black-eyed peas and rice—made his mouth water. Inside, men and women did the *snake-hips* and the *funky butt* to the music.

The room quieted down for a moment, and Willie glanced up, surprised to see the old guitarist motioning in his direction. He stood, kicking the stool behind him. *This is it.*

"Got a surprise for you folks," the guitarist said, trying to shout over the crowd noise. "This gentleman here is going to play a song with us. You all be kind, and give a listen to Mr. Willie Johnson."

"The man with two dick names," Jackwash called out. The crowd laughed nervously, and a few folks even clapped. Willie sighed with relief. *Thank you, my friend.*

"What do you want to play, suh?" the man asked when Willie joined him. No stage—just a clear space against the wall, away from the liquor and food.

"Something in A. Something fast."

The old guitarist nodded, looked back to the man seated at the drum behind him, and began strumming and humming. Willie stood still for a while, listening to the beat before playing. He held the guitar up on his chest, his eyes on the frets, except for a moment or two, when he scanned the crowd for a glimpse of Jackwash. He stood off to the left, away from the dancers, still holding the girl's hand.

Willie started simple, picking his way through two-string licks that would sing out over the sound of trundling feet. The guitarist started singing *Crow Jane*.

The old man had a high-pitched voice that did justice to Skip James. When he came to the break, he nodded at Willie and turned away, his fingers still framing the rhythm. Willie started off slow, but his notes had razors in them. His fingers trembled and shook over the strings, and beestings came out, cutting through the crowd noise. A few dancers had stopped to listen, so he pushed on, turning his simple lead into a runaway train, jamming note after note in and around the melody. The old guitarist stood with his mouth hanging open, but he and the drummer kept going. Willie doubled down, playing hammers and pull-offs in a staccato burst of music as if the guitar had become a Thompson machine gun, punching holes in the smoke and noise, laying waste to everyone in its path. He finished with a two-string bend and a slap across the neck of the guitar, and then—

Silence.

The drummer had stopped playing, and the dancers had stopped dancing. Someone in the back coughed. Jackwash put his hands together, and a few people clapped along with him. One big woman in front, dressed to the nines with a tiny purse on her arm, said, "That man has got the devil in him," with a touch of fear in her face.

"Yes ma'am, I do," Willie said, and walked off into the crowd. Remembering himself, he turned to thank the old guitarist. The poor fella stood with his mouth open, fingering his string tie.

"Damn," Jackwash said, grabbing his arm. "That was somethin'!" For just a moment, his smile disappeared, and he looked younger like he had when he was a boy. He shook Willie by the shoulders and hugged him. Luella stood to the side with her arms crossed. He searched her expression but didn't find the reaction he'd hoped for. Her eyes were on Jackwash.

After another two songs, the band took a break. The drummer, a young man wearing trousers and a vest—no shirt—drank water from a pitcher, downing half of it with his first long swallow. When he came up for air, he poured the rest over his head and then shook, spraying everyone nearby. The old guitarist stepped to the side, a small glass of moonshine in his hands. When a man came by with fried catfish wrapped in paper, the guitarist bowed, taking a nibble and another sip. The drummer shoved fish into his mouth like a sword swallower. Willie couldn't be sure if the man even chewed.

The fried cat smelled good—better than anything else in this mildewed sweatbox. But Willie was broke. No money, no fish.

When the guitarist finished eating, he pointed at Jackwash and the girl. Jackwash nodded and grabbed Luella by the arm. "Come on, girl. It's your time."

Willie watched, guitar in hand, as Luella sauntered up to where the band played. The guitarist hollered, but the crowd couldn't hear him— laughing and jostling each other, shouting to friends across the room, shouting for drinks, or just shouting for the hell of it. After the guitarist tried again, the drummer stuck a finger and thumb in the corners of his mouth and let out a piercing whistle.

When the room quieted, the guitarist said, "Y'all need to listen up. This pretty lady is going to sing a song, and I want you to pay attention." He turned to Luella. "You ready, sweetheart?" She nodded, and a change seemed to come over her with the sound of the first note. She unfolded her arms and dangled them at the side, her palms out. Her eyes widened. She tilted her head a little to the left and began to sing.

The first thing that struck Willie was the pitch of her voice—lower than he expected from such a slender little thing. She launched into *Any Woman's Blues,* with the guitarist picking *and* framing, doing a decent job of making up for the lack of a piano. The drummer brushed his fingers over the drum skin, giving the tune a classy, jazzy kind of touch.

Luella didn't slide away from the notes like Bessie Smith did. Instead, she hit the notes head-on, relying on the timbre of her voice, rich and resonant, to carry the song. The complex overtones of her vocals left Willie hanging on every note, trying to sort out the layers. And when she finally slid into a blue note, it sounded unique, as if she'd invented singing.

The juke crowd listened. No one danced.

She touched her neck with slender fingers and bowed her head as she sang. Her lips turned down, almost trembling, and by the time the song ended, he was in love.

The room exploded in applause. Mouth opened wide, she stammered her thanks and stepped away from the band. Willie tried to reach her with his congratulations, but the juke crowd engulfed her.

Disappointed, he reminded himself that she belonged to Jackwash. He shook his head and stepped to the side of the room, away from the rest. There, perched on a stool, the legend sat still, nodding his head.

Willie had to ask.

He walked up and blurted, "I've heard you play, man. You're the best." He'd forgotten to say hello. No matter—he plunged ahead. "It would mean a lot to me if you'd tell me what you thought of my playing." He set his guitar against the wall and stood back, waiting for the verdict.

The man on the stool had a long, narrow face with pronounced cheekbones that jutted out, like a chipmunk with a mouthful of acorns. He sang like a preacher—he'd either been one or would be one—and the whole delta knew his music. He squinted his eyes and stared for a moment, a wide smile splitting the lower half of his face. "Why, you played just fine, son."

"No, *really,*" Willie insisted. "I want to know what you thought."

The man's grin spread just a little wider.

"I *understand*, believe me," Willie said. "But I'd be grateful if you told me the truth."

The grin disappeared. The man squinted at him. "Ain't a race."

Willie waited. When the legend didn't say anything else, he said, "I don't understand."

"The blues ain't a race. Slow down, son."

Willie rocked back on his heels. Deep in his secret heart, he had expected the man to praise him. Or encourage him. He felt his face flush hot, and he balled his fists.

"Now, you have a genuine feel for the guitar—"

"No, that's okay," Willie said, turning away. He stomped off and then stopped. He'd left his guitar behind. He strutted back, sticking his face near the legend, making him flinch.

"Hey! What you doin'?" One of the other men came closer as if to break up a fight.

"You're wrong," Willie said, practically hissing. "You're *wrong*. It *is* a race. And I *won*."

Two sets of hands grabbed him from behind, dragging him back. He let himself be pulled away. "I'm all right, I'm all right. No problem here."

"You need to get out of here," a voice whispered in his ear. Jackwash! Willie relaxed.

"I'm going," Willie announced.

Four men, one of them as large as he was, escorted him through the door. The big boy, a field hand with forearms like briskets, said, "You in the wrong place. Git the hell out of here." He stuck his lower lip out and scowled.

"I need to get my guitar."

"You go now and be glad none of your arms and legs is broken."

Willie narrowed his gaze. "I get my box, or I don't go." He stepped closer to the big man and waited for the blows to fall. *Won't be the first time I've taken a beating.*

"I got your box," Jackwash called, trotting outside with the guitar. He put the instrument in Willie's hands, shoving him back in the same motion, putting himself between Willie and the other men. "Go on now."

Willie laughed, backing away. He held up the guitar. "Thanks, Jackwash. And thanks for tonight!"

"Don't thank me," Jackwash said, his expression falling. "This place ain't for you." He glanced to the side. The big field hand stared down at him.

Willie made his way around the cars that filled the field. Each car arrived full of people, and some of those people were spilling out of the juke to stare at him now. *Sorry, folks! No fight tonight!* He reached the road, laughing to himself. He thought of Luella. She wanted Jackwash more than Jackwash wanted her. Willie would keep an eye on that situation, and when his friend dumped the girl, he'd step in to *comfort* her.

The sun dropped over the horizon, and though the insects still swarmed, and heat still shimmered off the roadbed, Willie felt invigorated. *I played good tonight. Like a runaway train.* He whistled a tune, and the cicadas chirped the response to his call.

· · · · ·

1969
Fort Collins, Colorado
"How much?" Kennedy asked, disbelief in his voice.

The man at the front desk repeated the room rate.

"One night, please," Kennedy said, his voice cracking. *One night is all I can afford. Where am I going to stay for the next month? Not here, that's for sure.* He put his money on the counter.

The man handed him change and a key attached to a diamond-shaped piece of plastic. "Third floor," the man said. "Stairs back there."

Kennedy grabbed his duffel and headed for the stairs. He'd already walked halfway to the moon, looking for a cheap room. His legs hurt. This old place was the cheapest of the cheap, and he would have to skip dinner to pay for it.

Any plans of walking to Willie Johnson's place today had evaporated. All he wanted now was to wash the sweat off and lie down on cool sheets.

The room gave him another surprise. He'd known the place had historical significance. Perhaps people were smaller in the old days, because the room was like a closet. Hot air suffocated him. He put the duffel down, locked the door behind him, and headed for the window. The old wooden frame stuck fast. He struggled with the latch and frame for five minutes, finally giving up in a fury of sweat and exhaustion. A fly buzzed his head, and he swatted at it without success. "God damn it, fly, just stay out of my face!"

The room had a sink and toilet—both looking like something out of a museum. The porcelain was cracked and stained brown. Dripping, he stripped down to his boxers and used the one washcloth and towel to give himself a quick wash. Then he turned to the bed.

The corduroy bedspread had brown stains. He hadn't noticed them when first entering the room. He rubbed his eyes, leaning closer to be sure. *Bloodstains. There are bloodstains on the bedspread!* He grabbed the bedspread at the top and pulled the ugly thing off, leaving it in a pile at the foot of the bed. *Too hot for that in here anyway.*

He flopped onto the bed, lying on his back with his arms and legs outstretched. Within minutes, he'd soaked the top sheet with his sweat.

He tried the window again, to no avail.

I can't do this. They have to do something. No air conditioning? Is this the Middle Ages? Kennedy dressed himself in fresh clothes and headed downstairs. The front desk man was helping ruin someone else's night, so Kennedy had to wait in line.

When his turn came, he said, "The windows don't work."

The desk attendant sighed, his thin, sallow face taking on a pained expression. "The room was only partially renovated," he explained.

Kennedy frowned. "Interesting, because I didn't pay a partial room fee."

"I'm sorry for the inconvenience."

Kennedy waited a moment, hoping for more. When the desk attendant gave him nothing beyond a weak smile, Kennedy pressed on. "It's hot up there."

"You're on the third floor. Hot air rises."

He thinks I'm some kid he can push around. "No way. Get me another room."

"Unfortunately, the other rooms are either booked or under renovation."

Kennedy leaned forward. "Then I think you need to give me a discount."

"I don't believe I can sell management on a price reduction over a window."

"How about blood on the bedspread? Does that rate a discount?"

The desk attendant shrank a little, glancing around to see if anyone overheard. "Please lower your voice. I'll see what I can do."

Two minutes later, Kennedy headed back upstairs, a ten-dollar bill in his fist.

• • • • •

In the morning, he walked to Willie Johnson's house. He'd have taken a cab, if only for appearance's sake, but what if Willie was working? What if he was out? He couldn't squander his money like that. Besides, the map said he'd be crossing through Colorado State University, and he wanted to see what the campus looked like. Not to mention the college girls.

His legs were sore halfway across campus. The place was pretty, with huge flower beds and the mountains for a backdrop, but it was hard to enjoy the view. He couldn't remember when he'd done so much walking. His mom and dad used to drive him everywhere. Clearly, they'd done him a disservice. *Well, that'll change now.*

There were plenty of girls to look at along the way. Some of them dressed nice, with crisp blouses and skirts. A few wore sloppy clothes—hippies, he supposed. Two girls wore miniskirts, which was what the girls in Pittsburgh wore. Of course, Pittsburgh was a major city, so he couldn't expect that level of sophistication here.

He worried he wouldn't find his way, right up until the moment he reached Willie Johnson's house. The yard was a scorched mess, and the house looked like it hadn't had a paint job in two decades. Kennedy's dad painted his house back home every five years, and the yard was immaculate. Trimmed shrubs, flagstones, bird feeders—all that crap.

Please be home. Kennedy brushed his hair from his eyes, flattened his shirt, and tried hard to look older. Fortified, he knocked on the door.

No one answered.

He tried again. From inside, he thought he heard a muffled groan. He waited for as long as he could bear, and then knocked a third time.

The door swung open. "What?"

Kennedy cleared his throat. "My name is Kennedy Barnes. I'm a talent manager, here to see Mr. Willie Johnson."

"Okay." The man seemed half asleep or sick. His thin frame looked too fragile to hold him upright.

"Is Mr. Johnson here?"

"He sure as hell is."

Kennedy waited. The man at the door waited, too. Kennedy tried again. "Can I speak to him?"

"You *are* speaking to him."

Kennedy frowned. "You *can't* be Willie Johnson."

The man swallowed a laugh. "Why not?"

Kennedy stared. "Because," he said. "You're white."

CHAPTER FOUR: THE RAMSKELLER

"You got your hands in your pockets/ or maybe your hand's all up in mine."
~Willie Johnson, *Church Up the Road*

1969
Fort Collins, Colorado

Willie Johnson stared at the boy in his doorway. Wonder Bread boy, with round glasses and a tremolo voice. "I'm Willie Johnson," Willie said. "Least, I was this morning. What can I do for you?"

The boy stood, mouth open.

Willie cleared his throat. "Are you going to say something?"

The boy stuck out his hand. "Kennedy Barnes," he said. "Are you the Willie Johnson that recorded *Bitch Train*?"

Willie blinked. "Ah. You're from the Library of Congress?"

"Not exactly," Kennedy said, lowering his hand. "I'm a talent manager."

Willie tried not to laugh, and the swallowed impulse sounded like a cough. He went with that for a moment, rather than be rude. "Talent manager?" he asked.

"Yes. I'm here with a proposition for you."

Willie shrugged. "Might as well come in, then." He stepped back, opening the door wide. Kennedy took a few steps inside and looked around. "You aren't particular about the surroundings, are you?" Willie asked.

The boy looked around the room and then turned to Willie. "Maid's day off?"

Willie chuckled. The boy had some sass to him.

Kennedy walked to the couch and sat, gingerly, as if the battered piece of furniture might be ready to collapse. Apparently satisfied the couch wouldn't buckle, he stretched his feet out and leaned back. "Let's talk."

Willie chuckled again. He fetched a chair from the kitchen and planted himself near the couch. "I'm listening."

Kennedy cleared his throat. "You invented rock and roll twenty years before Chuck Berry."

Willie rolled his eyes.

"Do you still play guitar?" He glanced to the side, staring at Willie's Kalamazoo propped on the far wall.

"I play," Willie said. "What's your proposition?"

Kennedy bit his lip, and then, as if coming to a decision, he plowed ahead. "I'll buy us bus tickets to the Newport Folk Festival. You'll be discovered, and we'll sign a record contract."

Willie squinted. "What makes you think they'll let me play at your festival?"

Kennedy sat forward. "I've been calling George Wein. He runs the show in Newport. I'll set things up. Don't worry about that."

Willie rubbed his chin. The boy in front of him didn't seem old enough to shave, let alone handle musicians. But Willie had heard of the folk festival in Newport. Son House had been "discovered" there. Could the same thing happen for him? Truth be told, Willie had never even considered the idea. Play a festival? Why not? He didn't know anything about George Wein, but the boy seemed to know. "How did you get my address?" he asked. "And how do you know about *Bitch Train*?"

"You've been corresponding with the Library of Congress," Kennedy said.

"I sent them a letter. Is that it?"

Kennedy waved his hand as if the answer were self-evident. "I have contacts all over the United States. I'm always on the lookout for talent."

Willie stood and walked to the kitchen. "You want something to drink?" he called.

"What do you have?"

"Water."

Kennedy waited, expecting a second choice.

Willie returned with a jelly jar filled with tap water. "Here you go."

Kennedy took the glass, staring at it. "Flintstones." His voice was monotone.

"The glass is mostly clean," Willie joked. "Now tell me about the money. What kind of split are we talking?"

Kennedy looked up, glass in hand. "The usual split is—"

"Bullshit," Willie said.

"I didn't even say a number! How do you know what I'm going to say?" Kennedy's mouth hung open. "I'm only asking for twenty-five percent."

"Fifteen to twenty is the industry standard."

"Twenty percent then."

"And what are you offering in return? Are you paying our expenses?"

Kennedy swallowed. "I thought we'd each buy our own food on the bus ride."

Willie started to laugh again, but the boy was watching his every move, so he struggled for a straight face. "You think it's that easy? We play a gig, and get a contract, just like that?"

"Just like that."

"What happens if we don't get signed?"

Kennedy shook his head. "You're a piece of living history. You invented the music that changed the world. You'll be rich." The words rolled out of him. He'd clearly practiced this part of his pitch. As he spoke, he seemed to relax, sprawling out on the couch like a cat. "And I'll be rich right along with you."

Willie walked back to the kitchen. Dirty dishes filled the sink. The trash can by the refrigerator overflowed. He bent and pushed the garbage down to compact it, but the pizza box wouldn't bend, and the beer can on top tumbled out and hit the floor. He kicked the can aside and turned around.

By the sink, the cat's dish sat half-full. The cat had died a month earlier. He'd wrapped it up in a plastic bag and sent it out with the trash, but he couldn't bear to get rid of the dish. *Nikita*. He'd named the cat after a Russian girl he met on one of his trips to Denver. A working girl, with thick lips and thighs like a weight lifter.

He missed that cat.

"Can I help you with anything?" Kennedy called from the other room.

Willie closed his eyes. He had to work at the motel in the morning. And the morning after that, and the morning after that. And when he could no longer work—

"You still there?"

Willie returned to the living room, patting his back pocket for his wallet. "Come on," he said. "We're going into town. You have a car?"

"No," Kennedy said. "I walked here."

"Really? You're kidding, right?"

"I needed the exercise." Kennedy stood up and stretched.

"All right then," Willie said. "Let's go."

"Where are we going?"

"If we're going to talk business, we'll do it in a bar. Since you don't have a car, we'll go on campus. The Ramskeller is okay."

"Sounds good to me."

They walked at a brisk pace, Willie leading the way. Kennedy seemed to have a difficult time keeping up, so Willie pushed ahead. He'd walked this route nearly every day for five years—ever since being hired by the motel. And the boy was out of shape.

"You're a spry old bastard," Kennedy said, breaking into a trot to keep up.

Willie walked faster still. His thighs burned, but the look on Kennedy's face was worth the effort. Within fifteen minutes, they were at the Lory Student Center. The bar was in the basement.

The Ramskeller was a small, overpriced campus bar and cafeteria. Willie liked to order pitchers of Coors and watch the local musicians—mostly folk singers filled with angst and outrage over the Nixon administration. Their sincerity touched him. Once, he'd seen a young girl with straight blond hair singing Dylan songs, and thought she'd been special. When he returned a week later, she played again, clumsy chords and flat vocals, and he decided that the beer had been to blame for his bad judgment.

His favorite artist had been a man who sang and told jokes. His humor kept the audience engaged, but his music had bite. Protest songs weren't Willie's favorite, but this man's anger ran down his arms, into his fingers and onto the guitar strings. When he sang *Johnny, I Hardly Knew Ye*, the line about being "put with a bowl to beg" gave him chills.

Inside, Willie steered Kennedy to the bar and ordered a pitcher. "He's paying," he told the bartender. Kennedy gawked for a moment, and then fished some bills out of his pocket. The bartender asked for identification.

Kennedy shook his head, but Willie tapped his shoulder. "You're over eighteen, right?"

Kennedy fished his driver's license out of his wallet. The bartender gave it a cursory glance and turned to fill the pitcher. Kennedy paid and added a tip.

Willie smiled. A man who didn't tip was not to be trusted.

They took a two-seat booth and Kennedy poured beers. No music in the afternoon, so they could talk without shouting.

The bar's décor was institutional. Chairs with plastic seats and tables that wobbled. Old band posters decorated the pastel walls, along with various metal traffic signs, as if someone in a suit had decided that "the kids will like this." The overall effect was like a cafeteria. A cafeteria with beer.

Willie took a sip, swished it around in his mouth, and then swallowed. Satisfied, he took a deep drink, finishing half a pilsner glass in a single swallow. "You know, this town was dry forever. They just started serving hard liquor."

"Dry?"

"Nothing but three-two beer."

Kennedy frowned. "What's that?"

"This," Willie said, pointing at the pitcher. "Three-point-two percent alcohol. Beer for kids. You need to go to a liquor store to get regular beer."

Kennedy nodded. "I thought it tasted weak."

"You're a big beer drinker, are you?" Willie grinned and looked around the bar. "This is the first place to even have three-two on campus. Last year, a bunch of students held a protest, and the university knuckled under."

"Dry town," Kennedy said. "No whiskey?"

"Nope. If I wanted a taste, I had to get a friend to drive me elsewhere."

"Damn. That's no good."

Willie shrugged. "Depends. Some things are better off out of reach. Like a woman with a ring on her finger. Distance keeps you out of trouble." He paused, his face taking on a serious expression. "Okay, here's the deal. If we're going to do business, we're going to have to set some guidelines."

"Okay . . ."

"First. No bullshit."

"Sounds good."

"I said, no bullshit." Willie set his glass down and leaned forward, elbows on the table. "How old are you, son?"

"I'm twenty—"

"Bullshit."

Kennedy sat back, expressionless. Long seconds ticked off. On the other side of the room, a student played pinball, thrusting against the machine with his thighs to pump up the action on the bumpers. The bartender coughed.

"Okay," Kennedy said. "I'm eighteen."

"How many clients do you have?"

"One."

"What's his name?"

"Willie Johnson."

Willie snorted. "We'll see." He finished his beer and poured himself another. "Where are you from?"

"Pittsburgh."

"You like the blues?"

"Hell, yes."

"Who was Sleepy John?"

"John Estes. He recorded *Floating Bridge*. He was narcoleptic."

Willie frowned. "What's narcoleptic?"

"They called him Sleepy John because he had a condition. Made him sleep in the middle of the day. He could play, though."

Willie sat back, deep in thought. He kept staring at the boy, and to his credit, the boy kept staring back. "What does a white boy from Pittsburgh know about the blues?"

Kennedy smirked. "What does an old white guy living in Colorado know about it?"

Willie might have taken offense. Instead, he smiled and took another long sip of beer. He liked this boy. Young Kennedy had moxie. "Well," Willie said, "there's a story in that. I was a pup, no more than your age. Loved blues music. Loved gospel. Loved chants, shouts, and field songs. Loved it all." He slipped a folding knife from his pocket and began tapping the table with it as he spoke.

Kennedy cleared his throat. "You carry a knife?"

"You don't?" Willie asked, surprised.

Kennedy looked away.

Willie took another swallow of beer and continued. "I used to sneak off to the jukes just to listen. You could stand out back and hear the music through the walls. They wouldn't let me in, of course. White boy like me, and all. But you hang around long enough and pester the same folks long enough, and soon, you're running errands and helping to clean up. Sooner or later, you're a fixture. Like a chair. And if you sit in the corner with your mouth shut, they'll let you watch.

"And I had some help," he continued. "I had a friend who put in a good word for me with juke owners. Pretty soon, I made a name for myself, and folks didn't mind me hanging around and playing a little."

Willie finished the glass and poured a third. "My paps dug trenches for a living. Mean-ass man. Came home drunk, or angry, because he had a shitty life. My mother, God rest her soul, tried to keep clean clothes on us and food on the table. When Paps came home, he'd sit in his chair near the radio, planted like an apple tree, and we'd put dinner on the arm of that chair every night. Dinner at the left arm and whiskey on the right. And no one would say a God-damned word until he fell asleep, right there on his throne."

The bar was empty and quiet. Willie took another sip. "Am I boring you?"

"No." Kennedy put down his own beer long enough to shake his head.

"Where are you staying?"

Kennedy shrugged. "At a hotel in town."

"Can you afford that?"

"I'm okay."

"No bullshit, *or we don't go any further.*"

Kennedy closed his eyes. "Money is tight."

"Okay. You'll stay at my place."

Kennedy stared. "Does that mean we're going to do this?"

"We'll see," Willie said. He was silent for a minute, searching for the thread of the conversation that he'd dropped. "Here's the point. I had a taste for bad things, too. I liked hooch and I liked poon. I didn't do drugs, but most of the time, I had no problem with them that did. But the vice I loved more than any other was the blues."

Kennedy considered this. "How did your dad react?"

Willie narrowed his gaze until his eyes were slits. "Paps dug ditches. That's low. But not as low as niggers. He held that comforting thought close to his chest, like a passage of scripture." He sat back. "As for me, I was lower than the field niggers, because I was his son, and I liked their music. I was a traitor to my race."

Kennedy frowned. "Did he throw you out?"

Willie leaned forward again with his eyes wide. "Oh, hell no. He liked to keep me around. Bullies need victims."

"They sure do," Kennedy agreed, touching his tender eye. "So, you ran away?"

"Of course not. With me gone, he'd only have Mom to punish. So, I took his worst until I was old enough to hold my own. Then I beat him up. Beat him like a snare."

"Bet he left you alone after that."

Willie sighed. "No. He behaved himself for a few days, acting all polite. Even drank less than his usual. Smiled at me once or twice. I remember thinking that he was a nice enough guy when he was sober and all—that I would have liked to get to know him. He was my paps, after all. Blood counts for something. Then, one night, he crept into my room with a baseball bat and broke my collarbone and three ribs."

CHAPTER FIVE: GIUSEPPE'S

*"As soon as my feets hit the ground/
I'm getting out of this doggone town."*
~Willie Johnson, *Church Up the Road*

1969
Fort Collins, Colorado
When the bartender at the college bar gave last call, Willie shook his head and said, "Night's too young," before heading from the door to the streets. The old man was fast, keeping a walking pace just the wrong side of comfortable, so Kennedy had to push to keep up with him.

Ten minutes into the walk, Kennedy tired of the silence. "Where are we going?"

Willie didn't even glance back. "Can't be too particular, you being a young pup and all. We have to go to a place where your I.D. will get you a beer." He strode on, his hands jammed into his pockets. His limp put a hitch in his step, but his back remained rail-straight, shoes keeping a staccato beat on the sidewalk. They cut through campus, winding their way through old neighborhoods full of large, dark trees and broken sidewalks, emerging at the edge of the downtown district. From there, they made their way down Mountain Avenue, crossing the trolley tracks that ran down the center of the street, and arrived at Giuseppe's, an Italian pizza house and bar.

The interior looked like a warehouse, with long tables and gaudy overhead lighting. The music was cranked up over the student din. "You hungry?" Willie shouted. "They do a fine double-cheese pizza here."

Kennedy shook his head. He was hungry, but any pizza would be on him and his diminishing money roll.

As if reading his mind, Willie said, "I'll buy the next pitcher." He returned with a pitcher of Coors. "This is all they have. It's not good beer. More for kids trying to learn about real beer." He finished pouring Kennedy a glass. "Here you go, kid."

Kennedy took a big swallow. His head swam a little, so he shook it and took another sip.

"You all right?"

"I could do this all night," Kennedy answered.

Willie snorted.

The speakers blared out a new song. "That's Tony Joe White," Willie said. *"Polk Salad Annie."* He took a long draw from his pilsner glass, wiped his mouth with the back of his shirt, and nodded appreciatively. "Now, *that's* a good song. That ol' boy can sing."

Kennedy didn't recognize the tune, and apparently, neither did half the crowd, because the buzz of laughter and conversation went on uninterrupted. But when the next song came on—*Sugar, Sugar* by the Archies—everyone stopped to sing along. The sight of a hundred drunken college students singing the silly lyrics made Willie laugh, and then wince. "Sweet Jesus, not a lick of good taste here." He took another sip of beer, and his mouth turned down even more. "Nor in here," he said, pointing to the glass.

"I'd like to know what you think a good beer is," Kennedy said, leaning slightly to the side. "To me, this tastes like gold. Liquid gold."

"Urine is golden, son," Willie said.

Kennedy laughed. "You're a funny old guy." A lopsided grin spread across his face. "So, let's talk business. We're going to be rich. You know that, don't you?"

"I don't think we're getting anything sensible done tonight," Willie said. "Now, tomorrow, you need to call this Mr. Wein fella and see what's what." His gaze sharpened a little, and he added, "You have a lot of ideas and promises, but you need to know that I'm a man who judges others by what they *do*, not what they *say*."

"I will, I will," Kennedy promised. He took another drink. "I'm kind of hungry." He looked around. "What did you say about pizza?"

Willie glanced at his watch. "Might be too late for that," he said. "Almost last call here, too."

"Damn."

"Well, don't fret. The girls will be around with bread soon."

"What?"

"Bread. They cook it ahead, and if they don't sell it, they hand it out. Can't keep it overnight."

"Bread slices?"

Willie laughed. "No, not slices. Garlic bread. Don't they have pizza places in Pittsburgh?"

Kennedy became animated, his hands whirring and jumping with his words. "Oh yeah, they have the *best* pizza in the whole world there. My dad used to bring home Mineo's pizza with pepperoni and sausage, which was pretty funny, because Mineo's was right in the middle of a Jewish neighborhood, and Jews don't eat pork . . ." He started laughing and hiccupped. He clamped a hand over his mouth, trying to squelch the next hiccup and failed, which made him laugh harder.

"Settle down, little fella," Willie advised.

By the time he regained some control, a barmaid came by with an armful of bread baskets. "Would you boys like some bread?"

"Sure would, darlin'," Willie said.

She set a basket of bread down on the bench and moved on. Kennedy pulled back the paper liner, grabbed a piece of garlic toast, and took a bite. "Hey, this tastes good," he said. He chewed some more. "Great, actually. I mean it's garlic bread, but it's really good."

"Simple things can be good," Willie said.

"You're right. I like a lot of plain things. Peanut butter. Stew. Ice cream."

Willie shook his head. "Have another beer, kid."

"No, I'm serious. Plain things are good. You can live on them." He paused to drink again, as he'd been instructed. "When I came here from Pittsburgh, I lived on fruit pies—"

"Not exactly staples. When I was young, there were times all I had was grits or oatmeal—"

"I *hate* oatmeal," Kennedy said, his voice too loud. "Cream of Wheat is okay, but oatmeal? The stuff is shit."

Willie's face went blank. "Like you said, you can live on oatmeal."

Kennedy stopped short. He'd only known Willie Johnson for half a day, but he was pretty sure he'd just said something wrong. He kept his mouth shut for a few minutes, thinking things through. He recalled things that his father had said about the Great Depression and wondered if he had reminded Willie of his lean days. Old people were prickly about the Depression. They fed families of ten with a loaf of bread and other impossible shit like that. At last, Kennedy said, "Oatmeal is okay."

Willie ignored him, staring off into the distance.

After the staff cleared the glasses and pitchers off the tables, Willie and Kennedy headed for the door. "We have a walk ahead of us," he said. "Let's not dawdle. I have to work in the morning."

"You have to work?" Kennedy repeated. His tongue felt thick and sticky in his mouth.

"People work for a living, kid."

"What time?"

Willie glanced at his watch again. "We'll be home by two," he said. "I'm up at five-thirty."

"You're crazy!" Kennedy said.

Willie smiled for the first time in a while, though it was a narrow-eyed, sly sort of smile. "You'll be up, too. There's work to be done. Come on now." Kennedy followed him, shouting into a wind that had kicked up, asking him what he'd meant, but Willie's mind was on walking, not talking, and he didn't answer.

• • • • •

1928

Cruger, Mississippi

"Beefsteak," Willie said, staring at the grate they'd thrown over the fire.

"Nothin' but the best," Jackwash said.

"Ain't had beef in a long time," Willie admitted. He glanced up. Luella hovered at Jackwash's elbow, clinging to him like a fly on a plate of sticky buns. Jackwash beamed, a fork the size of his forearm in his hands.

Willie shuffled over to the picnic table and poured himself a cup of fresh lemonade. His mouth watered like a faucet, and he needed something in his stomach right away. The lemonade was cool and sweet, and he closed his eyes with the pleasure of it. *No beef in a while? No food at all.* If things kept up a certain way, he'd have to take on a job shoveling hay or some such thing.

Jackwash seemed to be doing better by a full measure. Always a sharp dressed man, he wore a fine, pin-striped shirt and pants with suspenders. Luella wore nice clothes, too. Jackwash had probably bought her the dress she wore, all ivory and lace. Willie wore bib overalls and a work shirt. He wished he'd given them a wash before coming over for supper.

Luella set out a tub of poke sallet—cooked greens made from pokeweed—and a loaf of bread. Jackwash put a stack of plates on the table and turned back to the beef charring over the fire. Bending closer, he reached in and speared a potato, transferring it to the top plate. "This 'un is done."

"They all ought to be done," Luella said, a little salt in her voice.

"You let me worry about it. Make sure Willie has some lemonade."

"He already helped himself." She glared at Willie as if he'd done something wrong. *Hell, I probably did.*

"Heard you got kicked out of that juke down by the river," Jackwash said. "That true?"

"Folks tell stories," Willie said. He *had* been kicked out though, before he even put a finger to the strings. A big fat apple-knocker didn't like seeing a white face in a black juke and proceeded to say so. Willie was lucky to escape with his guitar intact.

"Seems like you been kicked out of every juke in the state," Luella said. "White clubs don't like you, neither." Her dark eyes had a hint of the devil in them.

Willie sat back. "I didn't know you were following my music so close."

She snorted and turned away.

Jackwash dropped two more potatoes on the top plate and set it aside. Then he dropped the beefsteak on the next plate down on the stack. He stopped, staring at the table, shook his head and said, "Damn, Luella, ain't you brought out the corn liquor? This here's Willie Johnson we entertainin'. We got to get him wet, or he gonna dry out. He just like a fish—"

"A *whale*," she said.

Willie gave a good-natured laugh and reached for the steak. "This one's for me, right?"

"See what I mean?" Luella asked.

Jackwash slid onto the bench and put his elbows up on the table. "You can have 'bout half of that steak, there. Luella and I will split the other half." His smile turned sly. "You *is* getting bigger."

"Don't know how," Willie said. "Haven't had a bite to eat since yesterday morning, and that was nothing. An old biscuit." He sniffed. "I think my clothes hide my natural shape."

Luella had returned with the jug and three table napkins. "No," Luella said. "You're round, for sure."

"Well then, you best feed me, before I take a bite outta that skinny arm of yours."

Jackwash snatched the jug and took a swig, wincing. "Whoa! Now, that's how you celebrate."

"What are we celebrating?" Willie asked, still eyeing the beefsteak.

Jackwash turned to share a glance with Luella. Both of them smiled, like kids misbehaving in church. "Well, might as well tell you," Jackwash said. But rather than do so, he took up a knife and fork and cut the steak in two. He put the larger half on Willie's plate and then cut the other half again, giving the smallest piece to Luella.

Meanwhile, she put a potato on each plate and shoved the greens to the middle of the table. Willie reached for the jug and took a swig. Liquid fire burned its way down his throat, leaving hot embers in his stomach.

Luella finally sat down and took a small bite of greens. Willie waited until his patience had expired—a second or two—and said, "Come on now, spit it out."

Jackwash nodded, chewing his first bite of steak. "I could eat like this every day," he said. "And sometime soon, I'm gonna do just that."

"You find a dead banker somewhere?"

Jackwash snorted. "Sure did. You're eating his hindquarter."

Willie chewed. "No banker was never so useful as this is right now."

"Y'all are gonna make me sick," Luella said. She scrunched up her face as if she'd smelled something bad, which was impossible with the fire and the smell of beef and cooked greens floating through the air like a breath of heavenly perfume.

Jackwash chewed a while longer and then sat back. "You know I been running shine around here."

"Only reason the jukes let me in," Willie nodded.

"Well, that's fine for the short term. But I gotta think about the future." Luella leaned into him a little, and he corrected himself. "*We* gotta think about the future." He grabbed the jug and took a long draw. He patted his lips with a napkin and continued. "Did I ever tell you about my cousin Montgomery?"

"Once or twice," Willie said.

"Well, Montgomery runs a numbers game in Skokie. That's outside of Chicago. You run numbers up there, you come into some *real* money. Can't do nothing like that here." He paused, glancing at Luella again before continuing. "So, we gonna go up north. I got a place to stay till I get settled in. It's a sweet deal. I'm family, and Montgomery needs people he can trust."

Luella clutched his arm, smiling.

"Congratulations," Willie said. He belched.

"Now, don't fall all over yourself bein' happy for us." Jackwash frowned as if disappointed that his announcement hadn't yielded a bigger reaction.

"I'm happy," Willie said. He grabbed the jug.

Luella tilted her head. Her gaze narrowed, like a cat spotting a bird on the ground.

"Well, restrain yourself," Jackwash said. "There's more. You know, they got jukes up there. Fine ones—nothing like the ratty shacks down here. The best musicians in the world go to Chicago. And I . . ." He shot a glance at Luella. "We . . . was thinking you might come along."

Willie took a deep draw from the jug. His stomach roiled with the news, and he needed to shut that down—he couldn't let Jackwash know what he was feeling. If he was going to play the fool here, he'd do it as a drunk. He set the jug down, careful not to tip it, and then met Jackson Washington's gaze. "Bicycle only needs two wheels," he said.

"This ain't no *bicycle*," he scoffed. "This a damned *wagon*, and I'm the driver. I can pull all y'all to the promised land. You want to play your box where people can appreciate it? That's Chicago, man. You ain't going anywhere, playing for these broke down fools." His voice had taken on an edge, and his eyes were hot and bright. "You always told me you were going to end up in the city, playing for real money. I'm offering you a chance to do just that." He paused. "Unless our company's no good for your big dreams."

Willie shook his head. "You're my best friend. When are you leaving?"

"Tomorrow," Jackwash said. "You coming with us?"

"I'll let you know when the jug's empty," Willie said.

"You empty that jug, and you ain't gonna be in any shape to travel," Luella said.

Jackwash sighed, laughing. "That's Willie Johnson, there. If he was a train, wouldn't need no coal. Just hooch." He stood up, stretched, and stepped away. "Well, if we gonna make a night of it, I best keep the snake drained." He headed for the outhouse.

Silence. Luella frowned. "You going, ain't you Oats?"

"I hate it when you call me that."

She'd pulled her hair back and tied it off with a ribbon, leaving some free on either side to frame her face. She was thin, all angles, but when she smiled, the sharp edges softened. She hadn't impressed him much at first glance, but then he'd watched her sing, which changed everything. Looking at her now, Willie thought she might be the most beautiful woman he'd ever seen, either in magazines or in person.

Jackwash, who never stuck with the same gal for more than a few weeks, had been at her side for months now. He was still Jackwash, of course—playing with fire every time a fine brown thing showed some interest in him. But he seemed to really like Luella. She was smart—too damned smart—and they shared the same dreams. When he boasted, "I'm gonna be somebody," she nodded her head as if to make clear that she felt the same about herself. "*We*, Sugar. *We* gonna be somebody."

"Oats," she repeated. "Fits you, don't it? All plain and white—"

Willie waved her off and grabbed the jug.

"Why you mad?" she asked.

Staring into her eyes, it occurred to him that she knew well and good why he was mad. "Does Jackwash know you have your own little name for me?" he asked. "He's a jealous man, you know."

"I *know*. That man has to know where I been every minute of every day." She paused, honing her gaze like someone with a razor and a strop. "Now, you'd never treat me like that, would you Oats?"

"I'd take care of you," Willie said. The words slipped out by accident, as much to do with corn liquor as with the truth.

Her mouth dropped open for just a beat. "I bet you would," she said. She crossed her arms. "You ought to find you a good woman, Willie Johnson. I hate to see you alone. You need somebody who appreciates a steady man. Somebody who *wants* to be taken care of. Truth is, this butterfly needs somethin' more than that."

"You ain't no butterfly," he said. "A moth, maybe. A moth headed for the flame."

She snorted. "Sounds like a song. If you write it, I'll sing it."

Jackwash returned from the outhouse, patting his stomach. Though there wasn't a spare ounce of fat on the man, he said, "This belly o' mine is stuffed full, like a pig at a roast." He glanced up and took in their solemn faces. "What you two talking about?"

"Music," Willie said.

Jackwash smiled. "Figures. I guess I'm goin' to have to take up the harp or somethin', just to have somethin' to say around you two." He mimicked playing the harmonica, moaning through his fingers, and laughed. "So, you going with us, Willie?"

"He is," Luella said.

Jackwash sat down, grabbed the jug, sloshed it around to see how much was left, and took another drink. He started to send it back to Willie, but Luella grabbed it out of his hands and took a long, slow swallow.

Jackwash rubbed his lips. "Damn! Gotta love a woman who drinks like that."

Willie nodded. "Sure do."

CHAPTER SIX: THE RAMADA INN PUB

"One flick of the wrist/ he'll cut you a second smile."
~Willie Johnson, *Jackknife Blues*

1969
Fort Collins, Colorado

When Willie shook him awake, Kennedy sat upright on the couch. His head continued to move, though his body had stopped—or so it seemed.

"Not feeling so good, eh, little guy?" Willie wore a sleeveless undershirt and a pair of jeans. His feet were bare. "You gonna be sick?"

"No." Kennedy shook his head and then threw up in his lap.

"Ah, shit," Willie said, scurrying into the kitchen. "I'm getting a towel. Don't get anything on the couch."

Kennedy sat swaying. The stink covered his pants and the bottom of his shirt. Willie returned with a dish towel. "Scoop that mess into this towel and then throw it away." He bunched the towel up and tossed it across the room. The towel landed on the couch, next to Kennedy.

"I have to go to work," Willie said, pulling on a pair of socks. "While I'm gone, try to get hold of the Folk Festival people. And I need you to clean up the kitchen. Set all of the trash out by the curb—the truck will be by in an hour or so. Clean the dishes. When the sink's empty, wash your clothes off over the disposal. I don't want you messing up the bathtub. Then—"

"What the hell, Willie?"

Willie paused, the hint of a smile on his face. "I'm saving you hotel money, right?"

Kennedy tried to fix his gaze on Willie, despite the spinning room.

"Nothing free, kiddo. You want to manage me? Make my life a little easier. I'm the only one in this partnership making any green right now. You need to help out around here."

"But I'm sick!"

"Recreational flu. You'll live."

Kennedy looked down at the hot, tan mess in his lap. "Shit."

"Yup." Willie walked to the door and slipped his feet into his shoes. "When I come back, you'll have some good news for me." The words sounded like a threat.

When the door slammed, Kennedy sat back, staring at his pants. The acrid smell made him gag. He reached to his right and grabbed the dish towel. "How the hell am I supposed to do this?" He opened up the towel and tried to scoop the mess, but pushed it onto the couch instead. "Shit! I need a bigger towel! What am I supposed to do with this tiny thing? It's more washcloth than towel." He started to stand up, but that sent a river of vomit rolling down his pant leg.

When he'd done what he could with the dish towel, he put it in the kitchen trash on top the discarded pizza box. He stripped off his pants and shirt, leaving them in a pile on the kitchen floor. Then he turned to the sink—full of dirty dishes—and nearly cried. "Shitty old man! I'm not your damned maid!" He repeated the words several times as he filled a bucket from under the sink with soapy water, swabbed the couch cushions until they were clean, scrubbed the dishes, stacking them in the cupboards, and cleaned off the counters. He found a huge plastic lawn bag under the sink and filled it with the kitchen trash, careful not to touch the mess. Finally, he threw his discarded clothing into the sink, squirted green dish soap on them and turned on the hot water. By then, the sun was up, shooting its rays through the window like a spotlight.

"How am I supposed to haul the trash out in my underwear?" he asked. The refrigerator ticked. With no other answer at hand, Kennedy wandered down the hallway and into Willie's bedroom. The bed was made, tucked tight like a bed in a military academy, or he might have climbed in to sleep off the previous night. He checked the closet for something dry to wear, finding two blue denim work shirts, a pair of skinny Levi's and an ugly string tie draped around a coat hanger. Kennedy had two spare tee shirts in his duffel, but no pants. If Willie had been twenty pounds heavier, the pants would have fit. It was the old man's fault that Kennedy wouldn't get the trash to the curb in time.

Willie didn't have a home phone. Kennedy would have to wait until his pants were dry to go make his call to Wein. In the meantime, he was stuck doing Willie Johnson's bidding. "This isn't how Brian Epstein got started," Kennedy muttered. "And Willie ain't the Beatles."

Later, wearing a fresh shirt and damp pants, Kennedy walked to the nearest supermarket. He bought himself a candy bar with a five-dollar bill, asking for his change in quarters. The old woman at the register complied with a frown, which set Kennedy off again. All old people suck, he decided. *All* of them. Wrinkly-ass, crabby bastards and bitches.

Outside, he fed quarters into the pay phone, fully expecting the dodge from Wein's secretary like every call before, so he was shocked to find the call patched through.

"Mr. Wein?" he croaked. His voice was too high—he sounded like a kid. "Mr. Wein?" he repeated, dropping his pitch to sound like his father.

"You're the kid with the tape?"

"Yessir, I am. The tape comes from the Rankin archives. The date on the recording is 1934. That's two decades before Ike Turner's *Rocket 88*. My client—"

"And your client is?"

"Willie Johnson."

Silence. Kennedy shivered, though a warm sun was shining. "We're here in Colorado now, but we're ready to go east—"

"Willie Johnson is dead."

Kennedy stopped. His brain was still foggy, and he wasn't sure how to respond. "He drinks a lot for a dead man," he mumbled.

"Blind Willie Johnson. Preacher Willie. Died in 1945. Of syphilis."

Kennedy shook his head. "No, you don't—"

"Unless you've figured out how to raise the dead, you're wasting my time and my secretary's time."

Kennedy's stomach turned for the tenth time that morning. "Only one, huh?"

"Pardon?"

"Only one Willie Johnson allowed, right? Like there's only one Sonny Boy?"

More silence. Half the harmonica players in blues bands across America called themselves Sonny Boy.

"Listen here," Kennedy said, voice trembling. He had to think fast. The phone call was about to end. Willie's face came to mind, with his sharp gaze and sharper tongue, sweeping away Kennedy's moment of panic. He took a deep breath, pushed his round glasses back up on his nose, and smiled, imitating the old man's sarcastic drawl. "I'm not talking about some preacher who died twenty years ago. I'm talking about the great Willie Johnson, guitar master, who invented rock and roll in the middle of the Great Depression. And you have a chance to get credit for discovering him. Are you going to pass on that?" He bit his lip and pressed on. "You introduced Son House to the world. This is right up your alley. That's why we came to you."

"Let me put you on hold," Wein said.

Kennedy let go a breath he hadn't known he'd been holding and lay his head against the pay phone. "Hurry up," he whispered, "or I'll run out of quarters."

· · · · ·

Willie watched as Rodney leaned against the doorway arms folded in a studied version of casual. He chatted with Jessica while Willie loaded her cart with sheets and towels. Bending over, Willie caught a glimpse of the girl's tan legs. *Healthy girl.* There was no disguising Jessica's figure, despite the shapeless blue pastel uniform the motel required.

Rodney had certainly noticed.

"When I get my band going, you should come watch me play," Rodney said. He held up his left hand, mimicking fingers on a fretboard.

"I can tear it up. You'll see. Someday I'll have a record contract, and that will be it for places like this dump."

"Is that so?"

"You betcha. Not going to waste my time." He paused. "Not to say that I look down on folks working here. You? You're a young gal, just starting out. You won't be here for long. But this is no career. Gotta feel sorry for the folks who are stuck here for life."

"Did you clean out the dirty linen?" Willie asked.

Rodney frowned and pointed at the linen bag at the end of Jessica's cart. "It's right there," he said. "Help yourself."

Willie began pulling sheets out of the bag and stuffing them into his cart.

"Well, I have to get back to work," Jessica said. "These rooms aren't going to clean themselves."

Rodney shrugged. "Maybe I'll come by later this afternoon and help you finish up. We're real close to done at our end."

"Mrs. Simpson doesn't like us to work in teams," Jessica said. "She thinks we'll spend all our time talking."

Rodney snorted and rubbed the back of his fist across his mouth. "It's a sad day when people can't help each other on the job."

Willie started to push the cart ahead. Rodney's gaze followed him. "My partner's getting antsy," he said with a drawl, spinning out the last word as if it had four syllables instead of two. He pushed away from the door and sauntered down the carpeted hallway, trailing Willie and the cart. "I'm coming, old man," he called.

Willie stopped in front of the next maid's cart. "I'm here, Lenore."

"It's about time. I'm out of bath towels."

Willie reached into his rolling bin and pulled out a stack of towels. "You seem under the weather, Lenore. Is that back of yours bothering you?"

"My sciatica." Lenore's face puckered when she said the word.

Willie shook his head. "Growing old is a terrible thing."

Lenore put her hands on her hips and pressed, groaning. "I'm just tired." She looked up. "I'd be done that much sooner if you'd bring towels around on time."

"I'm sorry, darlin'," Willie said.

"We're here early," Rodney growled, arriving in time to chime in. "This is the two o'clock linen run, and it's one-forty."

"I wish I had more stock so you wouldn't have to wait," Willie told her. "I'm going to talk to the boss again today. It's not right to make you girls wait for your linens."

"Thank you, Willie," Lenore said. She paused to give Rodney a frown and then turned back to her cleaning.

Willie pulled the dirty linen from Lenore's cart and restocked the sheets and towels. Her trash bag was full, too, so he pulled the plastic bag, stacked it in his cart, and relined Lenore's basket. Glancing up at Rodney, he said, "You could help, you know."

"This here's a one-man job," Rodney said. "I don't know why they got two of us on this."

"You're supposed to be training. That half-day didn't do it, apparently."

"Shit," he said, drawing out the word again. "Training my ass. This place ain't NASA." Rodney shoved his hands in his pockets and rocked back on his heels. "I could do your job in half the time anyway."

Willie shrugged. "Let's get the dirty linen back to the chute and head down. There's towels and sheets to fold."

Rodney rolled his eyes and turned to go, his left hand playing the frets of his imaginary guitar again. Further down the hall, Willie paused at the top of the stairs to catch his breath, and Rodney sidled up beside him. Pointing down, he said, "Push me."

Willie stared. "What?"

"Push me down the stairs," Rodney repeated. "I'll sue this place. I heard the owner has deep pockets. I'll sue him, and sit on my ass for six months, writing songs." He turned to face Willie. "I'm serious. Push me. I won't say anything. Worst that can happen is a broken leg."

Willie pushed the cart instead. "Come on, kid. We have work to do."

Rodney followed, a scowl on his face. "All work and no play, Willie. You're a sad old—"

"And you're a lazy little fuck." Willie stopped and turned to face the boy. "You haven't done anything today but flap your pie hole."

Rodney's face flushed red. "What crawled up your ass, old man?" He stepped closer. "I've been doing plenty of work. For that matter, I've been carrying *you*, you old bag of bones."

Willie snorted. "You work like this when I'm not here, and the maids will run to Mrs. C. And you know what she'll do? She'll take a bite out my ass for not training you right."

Rodney laughed and began talking in falsetto. "Oh, no! Mrs. Simpson is going to yell at me."

"And when she does," Willie said, "I'll have you fired. You can go home and tell your momma why you can't hold on to a job."

Rodney's back went stiff. "Are you threatening me?"

"Of course I am. Are you stupid?"

Rodney took a deep breath and stepped closer still. "You need to watch out."

"Watch out for what, son?"

"*Son?*" The word seemed to infuriate him. "You're not my *dad*." Rodney reached up, his hand to Willie's throat. He pushed Willie's head back against the wall, using enough pressure to cut off his breath. "I don't like you, Willie. You're a crabby old fuck who thinks he's something. Well, you're not. One word to Mrs. Simpson, and you'll lose *your* precious job. I'll tell her what you call her, and you'll be out of here." He pushed on Willie's windpipe and then let up enough to let him talk. "Do we understand each other, old man?"

Willie's face was blank. "Watch your stomach."

"What, too close for comfort Willie?" The boy grinned. He still had him by the throat, so it was hard for Willie to look down, but when he did, Rodney followed his gaze. That's when he saw the knife.

Willie pushed the tip of the blade forward, and Rodney yelped. He backed up, bumping into Willie's cart, stumbling at the edge of the stairs. Willie caught him by the shirt and pulled him upright. "Watch yourself. You'll fall and break a leg."

"What the fuck? Are you crazy?" Rodney's eyes were wide with shock.

Willie laid the flat side of the knife blade against Rodney's chest, bending him back over the railing above the stairs. "This is my *cut-and-*

run. Know why they call it that? You get in a pinch, you cut. Then you run." He stepped back, folding the knife shut. "Some advice to take with you on your way out. You want to strong-arm someone? Make sure they're not carrying a weapon." He slipped the knife in his pocket. "Now, it's time for the run part of cut-and-run."

"What?" Rodney stood wavering in place with his mouth open.

"I said *run*, boy. I'll tell Mrs. C you weren't feeling well."

"But . . ." Rodney swallowed. "I'm not leaving."

Willie patted his pocket. "You are. Go on now. Come back to work when you got your head right."

• • • • •

"Kids today," Willie said.

The motel bartender nodded. He notched a finger behind his bow tie and tugged at his shirt collar. "I know what you mean. Had a new barback start last weekend. Kid wanted a break thirty minutes after he started. I hauled half of his cases for him and changed both kegs because his *back hurt*." He shook his head. "When I gave him his tips for the evening, he looked at the money like I dipped it in matt-shots."

"You give him his full share?" Willie asked.

The bartender smiled. "Yeah. Go on, tell me I'm a sucker."

Willie chuckled. "Spoiled little bastards."

"It's the education system," the bartender said. He pulled at his mustache. "Got university professors telling students this and that. Makes 'em soft in the head."

"Feeling that way myself," Willie said. "Give me a shot. I only have cash for one, so make it something good."

The bartender looked around. When he spoke again, his voice was low. "You know I can't. Against the rules."

Willie tapped the bar with his fingertip. "I know. But pour me one anyway. I'll be quick."

"What about Mrs. Simpson? She's already got a hard-on for you."

Willie nodded. "That she does. And her dick's longer than mine."

"Thicker, too."

Willie tapped the bar again. The bartender pulled a bottle off the top shelf and poured a shot of bourbon into a rocks glass. "Ice?" he asked.

Willie shook his head no and grabbed the glass, downing the shot in a single gulp. He winced and took a deep breath. "Damn!" The bartender searched his face and Willie smiled. "So that's what the good stuff tastes like? Smooth." He slapped a bill on the counter.

"I got this round," the bartender said.

"I know," Willie said. He tapped the bill. "That's for you." He stepped away from the barstool. 'Don't give it away to some kid."

They both laughed.

CHAPTER SEVEN: THE RIBEYE GRILL

"Save your advice 'cause it's too late/ ain't no mistakes I haven't made."
~Willie Johnson, *My Hard Head*

1969
Fort Collins, Colorado

Kennedy was at the door waiting when Willie came home. The house was clean, and Kennedy had to admit, he was proud of all the work he'd done. Willie came limping in like he didn't notice, pushing past to flop down on the couch.

"Well?" Kennedy asked.

"Well, what?" Willie glanced around the room, but when he saw Kennedy watching him, he stopped, closing his eyes.

He's not going to say a damned thing about the house. Okay, fine. I have news. Kennedy put his hands on his hips. "Aren't you going to ask?"

For a moment, it seemed as if Willie had dozed off. "I guess you got some news for me, then?" he mumbled.

"Damn right," Kennedy said, his voice cracking. "I spoke to Mr. George Wein himself today, and we're going to Newport."

Willie opened his eyes, startled. "Well, I'll be go to hell!"

"They're going to come by to meet you first, but it's pretty much set."

"George Wein is coming to Fort Collins?"

"Not exactly. His associate."

Willie's gaze narrowed and his lips pursed like he was going to say "bullshit," so Kennedy rushed ahead. "Wein's got men in the field all over the country, looking for talent. His best man is driving across Texas right now, and he's going to be here the day after tomorrow."

Willie seemed to consider this, his eyes a little wild like he'd seen the ghost of Robert Johnson crossing through his backyard.

"It's just a formality, Willie. He just needs to see . . ." Kennedy's voice trailed off.

"See what?"

"He needs to make sure . . ." Again, Kennedy's voice faltered. This was a thing he should have already cleared up. He'd asked if Willie still played the guitar, and Willie said he did, and there *was* a guitar sitting in the corner of the room, but Kennedy hadn't actually seen the man play. And Willie was old as bedrock. Could he still move those fingers? "He'll just want to hear you play a song or two."

Willie's face was blank.

"You know, to make sure you can play. You can play, can't you?"

Willie smiled.

"Okay, I was sure you could, and I told him so. But I haven't actually heard anything yet . . ."

"Fair is fair," Willie said. "We've had us a nice time, you and I, drinking a few beers. I got to tell a few stories, and that's a treat for an old fella living alone. But I didn't put much stock in our chances. Newport is a big deal, and you're just a kid." He stood and crossed the room to his guitar. "So, if you have doubts about me and this ol' box, I guess that's fair. Like I said before, action is more important than words." He returned to the couch, sat down, and began to tune up. The guitar sounded in tune to Kennedy, but Willie fiddled with the machine heads anyway. When he was finished, he looked up and said, "This song's called *Safe Haven*." He began to play, opening with a simple riff that sounded both familiar and fresh. The first two lines came at the end of the repeated riff, like a response to the guitar's call. The remaining lines followed the chords, like any 12-bar blues.

You really hurt me, baby.

You cut me to the bone.
Now I see you comin' round, wonderin' if the coast is clear.
You lookin' for safe haven? Won't find no safe haven here.

Willie's voice was stiff and pitted like lava rock. Kennedy liked the sound. A man with a voice like that had been places and seen things. A voice like that could be believed.

You say you sorry baby.
Mistakes was made.
Now you hopin' for some open arms? Well, let me make this very clear.
You lookin' for forgiveness? Won't find no forgiveness here.

Willie slid into a lead, playing bits of chords and two-string licks. When he made his second pass through the progression, he let loose with a burst of staccato notes. His old fingers galloped across the frets like a horse running in a familiar field. Kennedy shivered. When Willie returned to the top of the guitar neck, he repeated the riff that opened the song.

The past is the past.
You'll clean the mess you made.
With your eyes on tomorrow, you'll make a better world appear.
You're lookin' for redemption? Won't find no redemption here.

Then he stopped singing and looked up. "I'll play you more later on. But right now, we're going out to celebrate." He pulled himself from the couch with some difficulty and looked down at his clothing. "I'm going next door for a minute. Miss Jones has a phone. You wash up. You need to be ready to go when the taxi gets here."

"Taxi?" Kennedy's voice was stricken.

"I'm paying," Willie said. "Don't panic." He started for the door. "This is good news, and we're going to celebrate." At the door, he paused to look around. "Place looks good, too. Thanks."

· · · · ·

The Ribeye Grill was dark—so much so that Kennedy had to stop, hand to the wall, two steps inside. Willie moved ahead with some kind of old man magic, leaving him behind. The walls were covered in textured foam that came off in his fingers. He could hear the clink of glassware and the low murmur of voices. Cigarette smoke drifted out of the darkness like a fog.

"Are you coming or not?" Willie's voice seemed far away. Kennedy closed his eyes, hoping to acclimate himself. "It's fucking dark in here. I don't have bat sonar, you know."

A hand grabbed him by the shirtsleeve and pulled him ahead. A bar came into view, bathed in amber light from overhead lamps. An older woman wearing black-and-whites stood polishing glasses. She seemed attractive, particularly for a woman in her thirties. Kennedy sat on a stool, and Willie sat next to him, saying, "Hello, Tammy."

"Willie Johnson, you old reprobate. How are you?"

"Another day closer to riches beyond spending, darlin'. I want you to meet my nephew Kennedy, here from Pittsburgh."

"I didn't know you had people in Pittsburgh," Tammy smiled. Something about her reminded Kennedy of a tee shirt, fresh out of the dryer. Clear skin and a nice smile.

"He's the only one I claim," Willie said. "We're here for dinner, so bring us two ribeye steaks, mid-rare, with fries. Eye-talian dressing on the salads. A whiskey sour for me, and a beer for him. Might as well make it a Heineken. We're celebrating."

She nodded and turned to the back bar, grabbing a bottle of Black Velvet. Kennedy glanced at Willie, questioning, but Willie frowned, so he kept his mouth shut. A minute later, he had a beer and a glass, both chilled.

"She's pretty."

"Too old for you," Willie said, sipping his drink.

"I meant for you."

"Too young for me."

Kennedy leaned in closer, whispering. "Speaking of age, how come they didn't check my I.D.?" he asked.

"We're north of town. They ain't so particular."

Tammy came by and dropped off two salads. Kennedy looked at his in dismay. When she was gone, he asked, "Is that cereal on my salad?"

"Chex. Try it. Tastes good with greens."

"I don't like greens," Kennedy said. "Makes you shit pellets, like a rabbit."

Willie snorted into his drink and then burst into laughter. He shook his head and slapped the bar top. "You're a funny kid, you know that?"

Kennedy smiled into his beer.

The steaks arrived, fat and juicy, served sizzling on hot plates. The outsides were charred and beautiful. "Holy crap! That thing's huge."

Willie put a knife to his plate without comment.

"Good, too. Really good," Kennedy continued, his mouth full.

Willie gave him a sideways glance. "You act like you've never had a steak before."

"I haven't. Not like this."

"Is this where I get to hear what a poor kid you were growing up?"

"No, we had steaks. But Dad always grilled them to death. He could turn any meal into a puck. Like a pancake made out of meat."

"Cooking a steak more than mid-rare is a sin," Willie said.

"Tell my dad that." Kennedy chewed for a moment, and then added, "He said he worked in a slaughterhouse before he got on at the mill. Changed his feelings about beef."

"That'll do it," Willie said. "That's why I stay away from hospitals." Before Kennedy could ask what that meant, Willie waved at Tammy to get another round.

"Everything all right?" she asked.

"Great," Kennedy said. "The steak is incredible." He turned to Willie. "This place is terrific. Did you ever think of playing here? You know, a solo gig?"

Willie shook his head and spoke to Tammy. "Another round?"

"Sure," she said. "You play an instrument, Willie?"

"Play an instrument? Willie is one of the greatest guitar players in history. He invented . . ." Kennedy paused. Willie glowered at him.

"Invented guitars?" she guessed.

"I'm not *that* old," Willie snorted.

She patted his hand. "I'll get those drinks for you boys."

When she was gone, Kennedy swiveled on his barstool to face him. "You don't like to talk about yourself much, do you?"

"Easier to just listen and let others flap their jaws."

"But you were . . . are . . . a great musician—"

Willie's frown deepened. "I played the blues for a while. But I've done other things, too. I fought in the war, but I don't think of myself as a soldier. I work in a motel laundry, but I sure as hell don't think of myself as a laundryman." He took a sip of his drink. "What's your daddy do for a living?"

"He works in the mills."

"Pipefitter? Conductor?"

"Boilermaker." Kennedy stared at Willie with surprise. The old man apparently got around. How else would he know something about making steel?

"Boilermaker," Willie repeated. "Now, what about him? Do you think that's all he is? Not a husband? Not a father?"

"Not much of a father," Kennedy said, scowling.

"Let me tell you something. Your daddy was a boy once. Now he's shucking steel in the ugliest town in America. In between, he probably did a lot of things. Met a lot of people. He's not just a job, you know. Did he fight in the war?"

"I don't know. I think so."

Willie sighed and drained his glass, just as Tammy returned with round two.

"So, you play guitar, Willie?"

He waved his hand, but Kennedy interrupted. "Willie's going to play at the Newport Folk Festival this fall. We expect to get a record contract out of that." Her eyes widened. "I'm his manager," Kennedy added.

"His manager! Well, well!"

Kennedy rushed on, fueled by the beer. "You may not know this, but Willie was a famous bluesman during the Depression. They called him *Willie Johnson, the Man with Two Dick Names*."

Tammy let out a stifled laugh, almost a bark, and she covered her mouth with her hand.

"You'll have to forgive my nephew," Willie said. "Folks from Pittsburgh don't have regular manners."

"Well, you two are somethin'." She laughed again and moved over to a new customer at the far end of the bar.

"Why'd you tell her that?" Willie asked, a disgusted look on his face.

"It's a cool nickname, Willie. I wish I had a name as cool as yours."

"There's nothing wrong with your name."

"You're wrong there." Now, it was Kennedy's turn to frown. "You know what Kennedy means?" He didn't wait for an answer. "It means *misshapen head*. I'm serious, that's what it means. It's Gaelic."

"I don't get it. Your head's mostly round."

Kennedy set his fork down. His head was starting to swim a little from the beer. "And worse, my last name is Barnes. That means, *people who live in a barn*. I'm the misshapen-headed boy who lives in a barn." He stared down at the last of his steak. "You have two dicks. You win."

"Gaelic, huh? That's kind of cool, isn't it?"

Kennedy exhaled loudly and returned to his steak. "Who did you fight in the war? The Germans or the Japs?"

"I fought the Germans," he said. His voice had gone soft, and he spoke to his drink, rather than directly to Kennedy. The bar was draped in shadows, and Willie seemed to sink into them, as if he were hiding.

"You don't want to talk about it?"

"Don't want to talk about it." Willie reached into his pocket, pulled out his knife, and began tapping it on the bar top. The sound was a steady tap, tap until he began throwing in a few extra taps, like a drum fill.

"Are you mad at me for asking?"

Willie stopped tapping. "No, of course not."

"You kill anybody in the war?"

"I don't know," Willie said. "My eyes were closed most every time I fired my rifle." He turned. "No more questions about the war, son."

Kennedy nodded, staring at the knife.

Willie looked down as if surprised at what he had in his hand.

"You ever stab anyone?" Kennedy asked.

"Can't let it go, can you?" Willie shook his head. "Yes, I stabbed some folks. But not in the war. In Chicago."

"Chicago? When you followed your friend? Jackwash?"

"Yeah, Jackwash. He went up there to run numbers, and I figured I'd give them black-and-tan clubs a try." He stopped, scowling at Kennedy. "You're not going to let this go, are you?"

· · · · ·

1928

Chicago, Illinois

The dance hall was a renovated theater, with some of the original seating in the rear, still bolted to the floor. Up front, a wooden dance floor butted against the stage. The walls were draped from the vaulted ceiling to the concrete floor with dark, red velvet curtains that smelled of cigarettes and alcohol.

Colored patrons paid a cover charge to watch the acts, listen to the bands, and dance in the wings. The cabaret section, centered in front of the dance floor with the best view of the acts, was reserved for whites, who sat at tables and even braved the food menu. One peek inside the kitchen area was enough to convince Willie that he'd wait and have his supper at home.

Because the place was a cavern, the theater had an amplifier and microphone set up, center stage. The sound was uneven—the amp cut the top off the treble. Willie made a mental note to stay away from the top strings when he played his guitar.

He watched from the wings, his guitar in hand, as a shake dancer performed. She had a high yellow complexion, and her white costume contrasted nicely with her bare midriff. Her long sleeves had a fringe that ruffled like a bird's feathers when she moved her arms. "Impressive," Willie said.

"Pardon?" The stage manager, a squat white man wearing bifocals, stopped and folded his arms. He came up to Willie's chest and refused to look up when he spoke.

"She's impressive," Willie repeated.

"And who are you?"

Willie looked down at the top of the man's balding head. "I'm Willie Johnson."

"What are you doing here?"

Willie had his guitar by the neck. He lifted it straight up and said, "I play the blues."

The stage manager cocked his head and then, ever so slowly, lifted his gaze. "You play . . . the blues?"

"Sure do."

The man pursed his lips as he gave Willie the once-over. "Anybody ever tell you that you could pass?"

"Pass?"

"Pass. As a white man."

"I *am* a white man."

The stage manager did a double take. "Well, I'll be damned to hell!" He frowned. "What are *you* doing, playing colored music?"

"I like the songs," Willie said.

"Hmmmm. Well, watch yourself."

Willie shrugged. "I'm on my best behavior. I won't cause you any trouble."

"That ain't what I mean," the manager said. His gaze had dropped back down to chest-level, and he poked Willie in the sternum with an index finger. "Folks don't take kindly to people crossing lines. White boy playing the blues? Somebody might decide to teach you a lesson."

The warning came back to him as he strode on stage fifteen minutes later. He didn't bother chatting up the crowd. They'd already been told to give themselves a hand by the previous act, a comedienne who got nothing in return. "Tough room," Willie thought. He positioned himself close to the microphone and gave the guitar a quick strum. The sound was off, and for a moment, he wondered if he was still in tune, though he'd spent the previous five minutes making certain that he was. Electricity was not his friend.

He started with an eight-bar blues he'd written back home. The song was about avoiding work. The county had to hire extra help for a road project, and Willie needed the cash, so he took the job. Grueling labor. On the third day, rain put a temporary halt to the work, which did not bother him at all. He only went back to collect his pay.

Got me a biscuit.
Got me some bacon.
Sure do taste fine.
And if the sun won't come out today,
I got this jug o' mine.

Take you some corn.
Make you some liquor.
Just as sweet as wine.
And if the sun gonna hide all day,
I got this jug o' mine.

Hey mister foreman?
Why the long face?
God done give you a sign.
I'm gonna sit here under these eves
And work this jug o' mine.

He played the song with a slow, lazy shuffle rhythm, trying hard not to let the scratchy amplifier distract him. When he finished, he stepped back and looked up. No applause. No dancers. To his left, three black men stood scowling at the edge of the dance floor, arms folded. He smiled and nodded. When he waved, the biggest one let out a long, angry sigh.

"I see how this is gonna go," Willie said. The microphone didn't catch his words, and someone from the cabaret section called out, "Can't hear you!"

Willie's gaze narrowed, and he bent low to speak directly into the mike. "This next tune is called *Misery Train*. If this one doesn't fire you folks up, you already dead." The man at the table sat back, surprised. His wife, or his girlfriend, covered her mouth with a gloved hand.

Willie felt an old, familiar anger well up inside. These people didn't appreciate him. Fine. He let that insult fuel his playing. He imagined the anger pushing through his veins, into his fingers. He started out chugging slow, chunky barre chords, but by the second pass, he sped up, growling lyrics about being kicked out of his home like a dog, put out on the road without a nickel to call his own. Paps did that, and Mom never said a word to stop him. Willie let the song run away from him.

Back in Mississippi, they won't even miss me.
I'm gone, gone, gone, damned gone.

Then he stopped strumming altogether and began racing up and down the neck with a blues run, like a train at full throttle. The flurry of notes was too much for the microphone and amplifier, but that was okay, because the electronic spit and crackle seemed to suit the song just right. When his fingers got tired, he slipped back into his chording and sang the last verse again, finishing with a little hop and skip on stage, just for show.

Silence.

He glanced to his left, knowing that he shouldn't, just to see what the boys thought of his playing. The big one had a blank face, but the littlest one was shouting something at him, his lips twisted in anger. Grimacing, he pointed and drew a finger across his neck. Willie shrugged. If he'd had the chance, he'd have bought those boys a beer and tried to explain how much he loved the music. He had his own style. How could he be anyone but himself? He wasn't mocking anyone. But some folks took offense because it suited them to do so, and they wouldn't drink with Willie, no matter who paid.

Then, Willie looked to the wings.

The stage manager was motioning to him to leave the stage. *They're giving me the hook! Sons of bitches are giving me the hook!* He turned back to the crowd and bent over so he could speak directly into the microphone. "That's all I have for you," he said. "Y'all remember this. That's the best fucking guitar work you'll ever hear." He walked off stage to the sound of boos and catcalls.

Jackwash would be pissed at him. His friend had used his new connections to get this gig, and Willie had blown it. *Not my fault. Those morons wouldn't know good blues if it cleaned out their pantry and fucked their wife.* The angry thought made him laugh, and by then, he was standing in front of the stage manager, who clearly took umbrage at Willie's grin. "Ain't *funny*. I told you, some folks might be offended, and I'm one of them." He flipped Willie a single cartwheel.

Willie caught the silver dollar. "What's this?"

"That's your pay."

"This ain't what we agreed to. I'll take the bounce, but you're gonna pay me."

"That's what you're getting."

Willie stepped closer. The little man backed up, but Willie paced him. "You booked me for a week. Five shows a day, two bucks a show."

The manager pulled out another cartwheel. "Here, then. One show and done. Now, take a powder, wise guy."

Willie pocketed the money and headed for the side exit. There was no use arguing. If he hit the man, he'd end up in jail or worse. He gripped the neck of the guitar, choking it, and stepped into the alley. The sun was gone, and the air was cold and wet. *Fucking Chicago. I hate this place.*

Willie paused to calm himself, reluctant to leave. He needed the job. That little stage manager might realize he'd made a mistake and follow him out. There was a show bill to fill out, after all, and those manager types always turned their foul tempers on the next victim the moment something else went wrong, which was, in the entertainment business, every five minutes. He might realize that Willie wasn't the enemy. Might even rehire him.

When he realized the manager wasn't coming, Willie turned to walk out of the alley and found his path blocked by three familiar black men. The big one had his arms folded again. The little one had a straight razor in his hand. The third man eased back, glancing back at the mouth of the alley every few seconds.

"You gentlemen don't like the blues?" Willie's voice came out in a croak, and he cursed himself for the tremor that ran from his throat to his legs.

"Don't like some gray-skinned, ofay motherfucker playing our music."

Willie slipped a shaky hand inside his pocket, his eyes on the little shit with the razor. "I already shaved today."

"That's all right," the little one said with a thin, reedy voice. "You a raggedy-ass son of a bitch. You could use a second go."

The big one hadn't moved. He was probably used to winning fights on sheer strength. The little one, though, had taken some lumps before figuring out how to even things up with a weapon. Bad news.

Willie pulled out his knife. "Meet my cut-and-run," he said, flipping open the blade.

The little one eyed the knife and smiled broadly. "This gonna be some *serious* fun," he said, moving closer.

CHAPTER EIGHT: LORENZO'S PIZZA

"Ain't but one kind of blues and that consists between a male and female that's in love…"
~Son House

Kennedy sat on his barstool, silent, considering Willie's story. When he was younger, his father had explained, "I tend to believe a man until I catch him in a lie. Just one. Then, I question everything he says from then on." By now, Tammy the bartender had served another round, and his head was swimming. Willie went back to tapping the knife on the bar top, keeping rhythm with whatever song was in his head. The old man was always tapping or humming.

"So," Kennedy said after a while.

"So?"

"So, you expect me to believe that you fought off three men with a knife?"

Willie stared, as if he'd never considered such a thing. "No . . . what the hell? Are you an idiot?" He began to pull up his shirt, right there in the middle of the restaurant's bar, as if he were at home, alone. He pointed to a row of parallel scars running from his belly to his left side. "That little one with the razor cut me up. I spent the next four months flat on my back." He paused to take another sip of his drink. "That's when I got myself in some *real* trouble."

· · · · ·

1929
Chicago, Illinois

In the hospital, his world was an iron-frame bed and a wooden nightstand where the nurse put his meals. The good people of Chicago donated food to the hospital kitchen, so there was plenty to eat, but the late meal was always burned because the nurses cooked after the kitchen staff went home. He didn't hold a grudge over the scorch. The nurses were the only medical professionals he saw. Some of them were even nice. The fact that they couldn't cook didn't much matter.

One morning, Alice—an older nurse who was *not* one of the nice ones—brought a nurse-in-training with her. "This is Brandy. She'll be assisting me today. The patient in the bed next to Willie moaned as if to underline the introduction.

"He does that all night," Willie said.

Alice spoke directly to her charge. "You'll find that some of our poorer patients aren't appreciative of the charity they receive here." Brandy folded her hands in front and stared at her shoes.

"Not so," Willie said. "I was thinking you might have a doctor take a look at him. You do have doctors in this here hospital, don't you?"

Alice glared at him. To his fevered mind, her wrinkled scowl looked like a mask. "This is a public hospital. You are here because we don't turn patients away. In return, perhaps you can muster some silence."

"You bet," Willie said. "I won't even groan like I'm dying."

"Hmmm. We'll see about that," Alice said. "Time to change your bandages."

That night, dinner was a piece of charred meat drowned in ketchup. He had occasion to remember the meal because later on, the moaning man got louder—much louder—and in the absence of a nurse, Willie stumbled over to his bed to see if he could help. The man could barely keep still from the pain. When Willie drew back the sheet, he saw an open wound at the man's sternum, black and red like dinner had been.

When Brandy, the young nurse-in-training, finally came around, she explained that they had to keep the wound open so it could heal.

"That makes no sense," Willie said, and thereafter, Brandy ignored him when he tried to talk to her.

· · · · ·

When Luella came to take him home, Willie was glad to leave. Jackwash had agreed to let him stay at their place while he recovered. But recovery took much longer than he'd imagined.

The rib wounds healed into hard, angry scars. If not for the slash across his hip, he would have been on his feet in two weeks. But the hip festered, and Willie carried a fever into a second month. One evening, half awake, he overheard Luella whispering to Jackwash in the hall. "It's not good. The cut won't close, and it smells bad. He might lose that leg."

"Cut's on his hip," Jackwash said. "They can't remove that much leg without killing him."

"Can you get him something?"

"I gave him something."

"Not for the pain," she said, exasperation in her voice. "For the infection."

"Why don't you do some of that voodoo shit you always talking about." Good old Jackwash—always able to joke, whether or not his best, oldest friend was dying on the couch or not. In the other room, Willie tried to shift in place, but his hip screamed, and the blanket slipped down. The tiny apartment was hot, but not Mississippi hot, and Willie had fever chills. He rolled to his right as much as the wound would allow and tried to tuck the blanket behind him so that when he rolled back, he'd pin it in place.

"What're you doin'?" Luella demanded.

"Waiting for that sweet chariot to swing down here," Willie said, grimacing.

"Let me do that," she told him, fussing the blanket into place. "You hungry?"

"I am."

"Hmmm. No surprise there." A strand of hair dropped in front of her face as she bent over him. She looked like a schoolgirl.

Willie licked his lips. "You know what they say? Starve a cold, feed a fever."

"More like, feed a fever, grow a belly. Ain't no chariot could carry you into heaven, the way you eat." She glanced at Willie's stricken expression and laughed. "I'm just playin', Willie. You know I like to cook for you. Least you know how to say *thank you*." She said this last loud enough to carry down the hall, but Jackwash didn't answer.

Luella had been a surprisingly good nurse. On his own since he was a young boy, Willie was not comfortable with people taking care of him. But he didn't mind Luella's ministrations, even when she got out the washcloth and basin. Part of the reason had to do with how she went about her business as if everything was no big deal.

As days stretched into weeks, he depended on her without a second thought, even when she brought him the *gris-gris* bag. The little red flannel sack held a coin, a tiny bundle of sage, another herb and a bit of root he didn't recognize, a tiny magnet, a ring, and a page from a prayer book. "What's this for?" he asked.

"Seven items in the bag. Has to be an odd number, and seven is lucky."

"Okay, but what's it for?"

"It's for you," she answered.

After that, he just shut up.

When his convalescence moved into the third month, Jackwash came home with a beat-up six-string acoustic he'd picked up—a Kalamazoo. "Since those boys ran off with your other one when they laid you low," he said. "I been lookin' in pawn shops, in case I come across your old box. No luck there, but I made a deal on this'un. I figure you miss playin'."

The guitar had scratches all across the face. The neck bowed slightly, and the tuning heads were loose. Willie was so grateful, he could have cried—would have cried if it hadn't been Jackwash standing there with his big toothy grin. Willie played all afternoon and into the night, his back pressed into the corner of the couch for support. When, in the wee hours of the morning, Jackwash came home, he checked on Luella and came back shaking his head. "You know you kept her awake all night?"

"I didn't mind," Luella called from the bedroom.

"I'm sorry, Jackwash. I guess I couldn't get enough of it, after laying here so long. I missed playing."

Jackwash stood in the shadows, silent for a minute. When he spoke, his voice was soft and low. "I'm glad you like the guitar, Willie. Makes me wonder what it would be like to love something that much."

"You got Luella," Willie said.

Jackwash nodded, or at least Willie thought he did, and turned to his bedroom down the hall.

· · · · ·

By the fourth month, Willie saw signs that he'd overstayed his welcome. Luella still cared for him without a complaint, but she'd begun to laugh a little too loud at his jokes, and when they talked, the conversations were serious. She told him how she learned to sing from her grandmother. He heard about the first man to touch her—a nasty old cracker who owned the shack she'd grown up in. And he suffered through the story of her first true love—a boy who lived across the meadow. Willie hated meadow-boy just on principle. On more than one occasion, Willie and Luella stayed up talking until Jackwash came home from doing business, and lately, there was a look in his eyes that said Willie might need to move on to his next situation before long.

No storm or radio drama before he left. He planned two speeches, one for Jackwash and one for Luella. The latter consumed him. He imagined an intro that led into a poetic, melodic soliloquy, and perhaps an *outro* that ended with a kiss. In the end, he gave her a sheepish thanks and waved off the hug, shaking his head. She looked sad, but who could tell what that meant? Luella was a mystery.

That lost chance made his goodbye to Jackwash a little easier to face, but no easier to deliver. He found his friend on a street corner, standing under a lamppost with two other colored men. Jackwash towered over both, and it was clear they deferred to him by the way they shuffled and laughed, hands jammed into their pockets. That changed when Willie approached. Smiles turned sullen, eyes narrowed, and the hands came out of pockets, loose and jangling. "Jackwash," Willie called, but there was no welcome in his friend's eyes.

"What do you need, Jeff?" he asked.

"Name's Willie. You might have forgotten the last twenty years." He looked over at Jackwash's friends. "You remember their names?"

"Trouble and Mo."

"Mo?"

Jackwash smirked. "Mo Trouble."

Willie nodded and looked away. "I'm heading out."

For a moment, his friend's face softened. He grabbed Willie by the elbow and moved him away from the lamppost. "Where you goin'?"

"Home," Willie said.

"Mississippi?"

"Yeah. I think I wore out my welcome here."

"Nah, man, you always welcome—"

"In the clubs, I mean. I was tapped out before I got cut. I'm a little too white for this town." He glanced at the two men leaning on the lamppost. "A little too white for your friends, too."

Jackwash snorted. "Employees, you mean. Those boys help me move a little T." He stood up a little straighter, his chin jutting out. "Things are lookin' up for me here. I'm makin' a name for myself."

"Reefer's fine. You aren't moving *H* are you?"

"Don't like needles."

Willie shifted from one foot to the other. "Good. Stay away from that shit."

"You my daddy now?"

"No. I'm your friend." He stepped closer, arms spread out, but Jackwash backed away. Willie froze. Jackwash glanced back at the two men behind him and then back at Willie, his eyes wide with apology. He rolled his shoulders and asked, "You hear the news?"

"What news?" Willie's voice was flat.

"There's a kid on every corner, calling it out. Where you been? The stock market crashed." His voice became louder, clearer. "All those rich, white motherfuckers are jumping off rooftops. 'Bout time they find out about life on the down low. Serve 'em all right."

"Stock market crashed?"

"Wiped 'em all out. The worm turned." He grinned, glancing back at his companions. Then he stepped closer, voice soft again. "Speaking of money, you need some?"

"Nah. Figured I'd hobo home."

Jackwash pulled a small roll of bills from his pocket and shoved it in Willie's hand. "Take it," he said. When Willie started to protest, Jackwash pushed him away—the money still in Willie's hand. "You keep that hidden. You can't afford to have any more of your big white ass sliced off."

Willie looked at the money and then glanced at Jackwash's friends. "Okay," he said, tucking the roll into his pocket. Not as good as a hug, but better than nothing. "Thanks," he said, his voice practically a whisper. "I'll probably need this when the stock market thing spreads."

"What do you mean, spreads?"

"Shit rolls downhill," Willie said.

· · · · ·

1969

Fort Collins, Colorado

Kennedy concentrated on putting one foot in front of the other without tripping on a rock or tangling his foot in a clump of weeds. Walking in the dark was a hazardous business.

Rather than taxi home, Willie wanted to walk partway to town. A quarter mile up the road, they crossed over to the other side. There were no streetlights, and Kennedy was a little nervous about the traffic. Dark as it was, and fast as cars were going, no one would be able to spot them before knocking them fifty yards into a ditch. Willie chided him for his worry, but in the end, the old man was more vulnerable than he. Kennedy was used to ducking and running, and Willie moved like caterpillar across the asphalt. When they arrived at the other side of the divided highway, still alive and well, Kennedy breathed a sigh of relief.

"That's where we're going," he said. "Lorenzo's Pizza."

"Are you serious? We just had dinner."

"They sell beer by the pitcher. And they have a piano player name of Terry that I like to watch. Mostly does ragtime, but he'll play blues if I ask him to. Does a great version of *Nobody Knows You When You're Down and Out.*" He slapped Kennedy's shoulder. "Hey? I played with him once. My guitar and his piano. Sounded good."

"So, you really do still play? Gigs, I mean." Kennedy asked.

"I played for you tonight." Willie seemed momentarily angered, and Kennedy flinched in the dark. Anxious to change the subject, he settled on a question from earlier in the evening. "Remember when you said you left Chicago to 'hobo home'? What's that mean?"

Willie stopped dead. There was no sidewalk here—just fields and a ditch, and weeds as tall as their knees. He swayed a little and then shook his head. "You don't know *nothin'*, do you?"

"I know enough to ask when I don't know something."

Willie swallowed a laugh as if it had snuck up on him and tried to escape without his permission. He coughed a few times and then started walking again. Kennedy watched him go at first and then ran to catch up. "Well? Are you going to tell me?"

"I made it from Chicago to New Orleans riding the rails."

"Trains?" he asked, knowing the answer.

Willie continued, ignoring the question. "Took my time, too. I figured my heart was broken, so I was going to pout my way south. Didn't take long to decide that I was never going back to Cruger, Mississippi. Too many memories. Instead, I went to New Orleans to see what I could learn from them delta boys and take my guitar playing up a notch."

"Long way to go on a train," Kennedy said, remembering his bus trip to Colorado. "Did they have food cars back then?"

Willie stopped again. "Food cars?" He burst out laughing. "I'm talking freight trains, young fella."

"Less expensive?" Kennedy guessed.

"I didn't buy no tickets. I'd wait outside a train yard for something to come by and run alongside, looking for an open boxcar. When I found one, I'd hoist myself up, trying not to fall under the wheels."

Kennedy whistled. "That sounds dangerous."

"It was. I saw folks lose their legs on two different occasions."

By then, they'd reached the pizza place. Inside, Willie seated himself, motioning for Kennedy to follow. They took a table close to a small, elevated platform with a piano on top. The place was empty. The piano player sat at a corner table with a beer and a slice. When he saw Willie, he waved.

"What was that like?" Kennedy asked.

"What was what like?"

"Watching somebody's legs get cut off?"

"Well, you're all full of curiosity about certain topics, aren't you?" Willie paused in his reminiscence to order a pitcher and two glasses. Again, the waitress didn't ask for Kennedy's I.D. "We're still outside of town by about a half a block, if I remember right. Anyway, don't look a gift beer in the mouth."

"I won't. But what about the train wheels? Did the person's legs stop the train?"

"No," Willie said. "A train is a heavy piece of machinery. Those wheels cut through legbone like a knife through pie. Poor soul looks down, and whereas a second earlier, he had two legs, now he's got two stumps and he's bleeding to death."

Kennedy considered this.

"Why didn't you just get on the train in the train yard?"

"Dangerous as boarding a moving train is, the train yard was worse. Railroads didn't want a bunch of freeloaders, so they'd hire bulls to guard the train."

"Bulls? Like male cows?"

Willie waited to answer while the waitress delivered the beer. Kennedy tried to imagine a train yard full of freight cars, with a herd of bulls wandering the tracks. Didn't seem like the most efficient method of keeping the trains free of riders. When the waitress left, he asked again, "Bulls?"

"Not the hooved variety of bull. The railroads hired guards to keep hobos off the trains. Brutal, cruel men. Hobos called them *bulls*, 'cause if they caught a hobo, they'd stomp him to a pulp. Or kill him."

"Why?"

"Keep hobos—men like me—off the trains."

"Were there a lot of hobos?"

Willie nodded. "Longer the Depression went on, the more of them there were. Most of them just wanted work, and the trains were the only real way to get to where the work was. For others, hoboing was a choice. A way of life. Some folks still make that choice, though it's getting harder to get on a train." He emptied his glass. Some of the beer had trickled onto his chin, though he didn't seem to notice. "My hip was still a mess, and I had the guitar Jackwash gave me, so getting into a boxcar was a problem. But an open door usually meant someone was already in the boxcar, which meant that I'd get a helping hand."

"I'm surprised they didn't steal your guitar and push you back out."

"No," Willie said. "It wasn't like that. Folks took care of each other back then. There wasn't much crime to speak of. Everyone was hurting, so nobody wanted to make things worse for anyone else. People respected each other's property."

"How long did it take you to get to New Orleans?"

"Don't recall. But I rode the rails for a few years, all told. I'd play here and there, and when folks got tired of me, I'd move on."

"Sounds like a hard life."

Willie waved him off. "Nah. Always had a little food 'cause people shared. And there were always hobo jungles, so you'd have a place to sleep."

"Hobo jungle?"

"What do they teach you in school?" Willie said, his face screwed up in dismay. "What did they tell you about the Depression?"

"Started with the stock market crash, lasted for years until Franklin Delano Roosevelt saved the country with work programs."

"Okay," Willie said. "Now *that's* the stupidest thing you've said tonight. The new stupidest thing."

The piano player, who'd climbed up to start his next set, pointed at Willie and began to play a blues tune. He wore a white ruffled shirt, tight red vest and red bow tie in keeping with the wait staff and the general décor of the restaurant, which was stuffed with old time mementos and bric-a-brac. The piano, a bit out of tune, had a bright, tinny sound that filled the empty room. Kennedy shook his head. "That doesn't sound good—"

"Shut it," Willie said. "The man is playing."

· · · · ·

Mercifully, Willie did not want to walk home. Kennedy dozed in the cab and was ready to go straight to bed when they reached Willie's house, but the old man grabbed his guitar. Watching the piano player had evidently put an itch in his fingers. Kennedy settled onto the couch and listened.

Willie played a few blues standards before grabbing a bottle from the kitchen. He returned, swaying, and sat down to play again. They'd both had far too much to drink already. Kennedy's head swam as he watched Willie swallow something amber, straight from the bottle.

"I play this one for you yet?" he asked, launching into *Safe Haven* again.

"Yeah, I heard that one already. It's good. Really good." Kennedy tried to stand up, but he was unsteady, and the couch seemed to have swallowed the lower half of his body.

"This, then." Willie began to play, and Kennedy froze.

The song wasn't blues—not really—though it had some blue notes. Jazz? He couldn't tell. Jazz never seemed to have a strong enough melody, but this song had one. A sad, winding melody that rolled downward, settling and seeping into his bones. Kennedy sat back, his eyes closed, tears forming at the corners of his eyes.

When it was silent again, he looked at Willie. "You didn't sing."

"No words."

"What's that called?"

"*Sins in Blue.*"

"Beautiful song. Saddest thing I've ever heard."

Willie nodded and took another drink.

"What's it about?"

Willie started to speak but took still another sip from the bottle instead. Finally, he said, "It's in the title. It's about sin."

"Your sins?"

Willie nodded, his eyes hard and dark.

"Was it something you did in the war?"

"No. I already told you. I don't have any stories for you about killing some Nazi, or a squad of Nazis."

"What then?" Kennedy pressed. "What's a sin, anyway? I know what my father would say. He thinks not going to church is a sin."

Willie eyed him like he was a snake.

"Willie?"

Willie tried to set down the bottle, and it tipped over. He snatched it up and wiped the spill with his stocking feet, smearing the liquor over the carpet. "When I was a boy," he said, "my pap said it was a sin to spill good liquor."

Kennedy laughed.

"Of course, down at the Washing the Disciple's Feet Resurrection Ministries, the church ladies were happy to tell me that the *blues* was a sin."

"Did you believe them?"

"Part of me did. The part that wanted to raise hell."

"Do you think it's a sin now?"

"No, of course not." Wille looked down, openmouthed, as if he'd just realized he still had his guitar in his lap. He stood and put the guitar in the corner with exaggerated caution as if he were stacking plate glass against the wall. Kennedy was sure he'd forgotten the conversation when Willie picked up where he'd left off. "No, sin is something much uglier." His voice was old and wet. He coughed.

Kennedy shivered. "What did you do?"

"I killed someone. I killed someone I loved." He paused. "Now, *that's* a sin."

CHAPTER NINE: THE SUGAR CANE TWELVE

"Even the angels dance with the devil/
Tryin' to keep warm in this cold, cold town."
~Willie Johnson, *Chicago Blues*

1969
Fort Collins, Colorado
Kennedy spent the night on the couch. His back hurt from sleeping wrong, and it took him nearly an hour to get moving. An angry fly, alternating between the windowpane and Kennedy's face, finally convinced him to stand and scratch. He checked Willie's bedroom and found the bed empty. Had he gone to work? Kennedy sang to himself as he headed for the bathroom.

Woke up this mornin', and my Willie Johnson was gone.

Standing over the toilet, Kennedy glanced down. "Only one of you, little fella," he said. "*Not two. One will have to do.*" When he laughed, his head throbbed like someone had just used a two-by-four on him in anger.

How in hell did that old man drink like he did without keeling over?

Then Kennedy remembered Willie's late-night confession. Had he really killed someone? Who had he killed? He said he'd killed someone he loved.

Time for chores. Pushing a washcloth across the kitchen counter as if to clean, Kennedy decided that Willie must have killed Jackwash. He didn't know all the story yet, but those two had been on a collision course. Two men loving the same woman was enough to blow up any friendship. There were a hundred blues songs written about that very thing. But murder? Damn!

Of course, Willie hadn't said anything about *murder*. He said he'd *killed* someone. Maybe it was self-defense.

More flies buzzed against the window over the kitchen sink. Kennedy rolled a dish towel and began swatting the insects, missing them for the most part. One swing caught the small cactus plant in a clay pot that Willie had put on the sill, sending it crashing into the sink. Kennedy stared at the pot shards and spilled dirt, wondering how to undo the mess. He scooped everything up with the dish towel and dumped it into the trash can. *Willie knows I'm a clumsy kid. He won't be surprised.* The thought made him smile. Willie wouldn't hold the damage against him. It was just a half-dead looking cactus anyway. Kennedy's dad would have gone ballistic over his clumsiness. He'd have given him the old speech about accidents: "You don't swing your arms around at the kitchen table and then tell me the spilled milk was an accident."

Doesn't mean he didn't love you.

The thought made him wince. He hadn't even called home to say he was okay. That was wrong. He needed to call.

Kennedy shook his head as if to jostle the thought out of his mind. *First, I need to straighten this place up. Our future starts tomorrow.*

The living room was a mess, even though Kennedy had cleaned up the day before. Sometime after coming home from the pizza place, they'd managed to trash everything again. Kennedy wanted to lay back down on the couch.

Instead, he kept working. He imagined where the Newport agent and Willie would sit. Then he began moving furniture. He'd promised Willie he would be his manager. Said he'd look after his interests. Talk was cheap. *Get to work*, he thought.

· · · · ·

When Willie came home, a bag in hand, Kennedy was at the door. "I cleaned up again. All ready to meet the Newport guy. Where are we going tonight?"

"Nowhere. I want to run through some songs and then get to bed early." Willie looked tired. The lines on his face were deeper, and the skin under his eyes was an unhealthy combination of gray and yellow.

"You could use a good night's sleep."

"For the last three decades," Willie agreed.

"What's for dinner, then?"

Willie pointed at the bag. "I grabbed some to-go from the Pancho Café. You like Mexican food?"

"I don't know," Kennedy said. His face was probably saying *no*. He didn't like trying new things.

"Time to expand your horizons," Willie said.

For the first time since Kennedy had come to Fort Collins, they sat down for a meal at home, settling down at a small Formica table with legs painted the same off-yellow as the kitchen walls. Willie groaned as he sat, the pain evident in his face.

"Your hip?"

Willie nodded, keeping his lips pressed tight.

"So, it never healed after you got cut?"

Willie seemed perplexed for a moment. "Oh. No, that eventually healed. The war did my hip in."

Kennedy leaned forward. "You were wounded in the war?"

Willie closed his eyes. "No."

"Sorry I asked."

"Don't worry about it." Willie took a Styrofoam container out of the bag and shoved it across the table. Kennedy popped the lid and stared.

"It's a burrito."

"How can you tell?" The thing was smothered in red sauce and cheese and topped with shredded lettuce that slid to the side, collecting in one corner.

"Because I ordered burritos. Now, eat. I paid for that."

Willie fished a pair of plastic forks out of the bag and passed one over. Then he opened his dinner and began to shovel food into his mouth.

"When you have time to take a breath," Kennedy said, "tell me how you injured your hip. I'm curious."

Willie stared at him while he chewed.

"I don't get it," Kennedy said. "You're all full of stories, but you don't want to talk about things that interest me."

"War?"

"Well, yeah."

Willie swallowed his food. "Hate to disappoint you. I was on my way to pick up supplies, and the dumb-ass driver rolled the jeep."

"What happened to him?"

"He injured his hip," Willie said.

Kennedy considered this for a moment.

Willie shook his head, a rueful smile on his face. "I was the dumb-ass driver, Kennedy."

"Oh."

"You can see why I don't want to talk about it."

"Sure, sure." Kennedy tried to cut through the burrito with the plastic fork, but the utensil bent and snapped. "So, what was—" He stopped. He wanted to ask about killing Jackwash, but Willie wouldn't talk about that unless he was plenty drunk. "What was the Great Depression like?" he asked instead. "I mean, what was it like, uh, day-to-day?"

"Depressing." Willie finished the last of his burrito and pushed the container away. "I was on the move most of the time. Slept nights in jungles. No rent. Most often, I ate and slept with the coloreds. That's where I was comfortable. But I wasn't always welcome there, and once I made my preference known, I wasn't much welcome with the whites either."

"That's bullshit," Kennedy said, drawing out the curse word. He walked to the kitchen drawers and pulled out a metal fork. "So, nobody liked you?"

"Wasn't like *that*," Willie said. "Nobody chased anybody out of a jungle. Folks on the road have a code. Besides, I could always pull out my guitar and play a few tunes, so folks tolerated me. Earned myself many a dinner that way. A cup of stew, hoecakes—"

"Hoecakes?"

"Cornmeal, water, and a pinch of salt, stirred and fried in fat."

"What kind of name is hoecakes?"

"Story goes that slaves used to cook them on a greased garden hoe over a fire. Fried the cakes on the blade. Seen it done that way once or twice. But the story's mostly wrong. Hoe is an old name for griddle."

"Doesn't sound all that tasty."

"It wasn't. A hobo friend used to call the mixture the *batter of hopelessness*." He laughed. "But the real hopelessness is an empty stomach."

Kennedy considered this while revisiting his burrito. Wasn't bad, really. Lots of cheese, which was good. As he chewed, he wondered how to ask Willie about Jackwash. Then he thought of an easier question.

"After you left Chicago, did you ever see Jackwash and Luella again?"

Willie looked away. "Yes."

"Did they come south, or something?"

"No. After a few years, I got it in my mind to go see how they were doing. I'd gone home by then, staying with an aunt. Aunt Beatrice. Stern old biddy. Wouldn't let me play music inside the house. Thought I'd be inviting the devil in. Anyway, I wrote Jackwash a letter and said I'd be passing through Chicago. He wrote back—or Luella wrote the letter for him—sayin' come on up. I hit the rails that very night. I wondered if maybe the bloom had gone off their rose, and maybe I'd have a chance to step in."

"You still loved her?"

The only hint that Kennedy had of the emotion behind the answer was a slight trembling of the shoulders.

· · · · ·

1931

Chicago, Illinois

The Sugar Cane Twelve was a private membership club. A dozen men of means in the community, including a few black doctors, lawyers, and businessmen, had pooled their resources and formed a social club that held parties and charged admission. Patrons could dance, drink, and listen to music in an upscale setting that spoke of money, from the bruiser in the tux at the front door to the cigarette girls, dressed in red velvet. Willie had shown up in his road overalls, but Jackwash told him not to worry. "Nobody care 'bout your clothes, Willie."

Luella, who'd been cool to him since his arrival, said, "You dressed like the ragman." Willie knew she wasn't joking, and her observation shriveled him.

Inside the club, Willie saw mostly black faces. He'd been used to mixed company on the road, but this crowd was a different sort. "Lot of money in this room," he whispered to Jackwash.

"Sure you're right," Jackwash said. "And every upper shady in this town knows my name, I can tell you that. They know I'm an up-and-comer."

"I'm not dressed right."

"They'd have stopped you at the door twice—once for lookin' like a sharecropper and once for that face of yours."

Willie frowned. "Why am I here, then?"

Jackwash leaned in close. "You're here with *me*," he said. "You got no worries."

Willie began to worry.

Luella, who had slipped away the moment they'd entered the club, returned with two drinks. She handed one to Jackwash. "I was gonna buy three, but I only got two hands. Besides, I don't know what Willie's drinking these days. You been hobo'n so long, you might prefer Sterno." She laughed then, her eyes glistening, and Willie felt his heart sink. She was more beautiful than ever, but her personality had taken on a sharp edge. Her humor always carried a bite, but Willie imagined that was a cover her vulnerability. Now, she seemed carefree and a little bit cruel. That's when he noticed the marks on her arm.

Two men jostled Willie from behind as they passed, and Willie stepped closer to Jackwash. "This place is crowded. I thought it was private membership only."

"It is," Jackwash said. His face had filled out a bit, and his belt was a little tight. The Chicago highlife had apparently been good to him. "Everybody here pays ten dollars to be a member. Money ain't picky, and these people like to be a part of what's goin' on." He nodded in the direction of a nearby table. "See that fella? He's a ward boss. The man with him—the one with the fat, checkered tie? He's carrying a roll of bills in his pocket thick as a slab of bacon." He tightened his grip on Willie's arm. "None of these peoples been eatin' Hoover stew, that's for sure."

Willie winced. Many a night, he'd been grateful for a ladle of thin broth, hot dog slices and whatever vegetables had been scrounged up to finish the recipe. He shrank in place, feeling ashamed for some reason. *No reason to feel this way. I'm with friends.* He stuck his chin out as if nothing could bother him. "You're a member?"

"Hell, I'm practically the thirteenth sugar cane. Ain't a single person here that don't know Jackson Washington."

"Still running numbers?"

"Nah, the new game is policy, and that's left to the neighborhoods. They hold drawings a couple times a day. Policy collectors use the money to keep their families floating, and that's good for them, you know?"

"How you getting your money, then?" Willie asked. He thought of the marks on Luella's arm.

"Little of this, an' a little of that. Why you so curious? Gonna hit me for a loan?"

Willie shrugged. A patron passing by stopped to glare at Willie, nod at Jackwash, and then move on. At the front of the room, the band had assembled. They had a saxophone and a trombone player, along with the usual piano, bass, guitarist and drummer. "Who are these guys?" Willie asked.

"Some territory band," Jackwash said. "Must be hard up. They takin' one night here instead of a week at an Elks club." He glared at the singer—a slender girl with buck teeth and high yellow skin. "Bet she can't sing none. Bet Luella could blow her off the stage."

"What about Luella? Is she singing anywhere?"

Jackwash shook his head. "No."

"Why not?" Willie insisted.

"She goin' through something. She'll get over it." He glared at Willie. "Don't worry about her. I'm takin' care of her jus' fine."

Willie tried to focus on the band. They were dressed in fine evening clothes, smiling at each other, and laughing. What would it be like to be a part of a band like that? He stared at the guitarist, dressed in a jacket, and then looked down at his overalls. He had no business being here in this nice club. What was he thinking?

When he glanced right, Jackwash was gone. A surly man in a black Fedora had taken his place. The man was tall—if Willie took him in at eye-level, he'd be staring at the man's chest. Stubborn, Willie refused to look up.

"What you lookin' at? You lookin' at my buttons?"

"I'm not looking. I'm thinking."

"What you thinkin 'bout?"

"I'm thinking there aren't a lot of white boys in this room," Willie said.

"There's *you*."

There were other white men in the club, but not many. Willie took a deep breath. Where was Jackwash?

The tall man moved closer, and Willie readied himself. He could smell whiskey on the man's breath. Luckily, Jackwash chose that moment to return, a drink in his hand. "Moe Brown!" he said as if he'd come upon a beloved cousin. "I see you met my friend, Willie Johnson. Willie here's a musician."

The man scowled. "Why you hanging with this piece of trash?" Willie took the drink from Jackwash and downed half of it in a single gulp.

The band started, giving Willie something to focus on besides being singled out. They covered an array of radio hits, sticking to standard arrangements, but they weren't afraid to throw in a touch of their own to add to the musical gumbo. He liked the way the members of the band played off each other. A bass line led to a countermelody, and he mentally tucked the phrase away for future use. Later, he'd pick the notes out on his guitar, and think about how to put them to use.

The sax player was particularly good. Willie tapped Jackwash on the shoulder and said, "That fella knows his way around a gobble-pipe."

Jackwash nodded. "Brother can blow."

Territory bands were falling on hard times because of the Depression. He hoped these fellows were able to keep going. Them and their one little skinny gal.

Like Luella. The thought of her sent a shiver down his backbone. He looked around the room, unable to spot her in the crush of patrons. He hadn't seen her in two years. He wanted to talk to her, to connect like they had when she'd nursed him back to health.

She flitted past while the band played their version of *Love Letters in the Sand,* waving on her way to the other side of the room. The girl onstage couldn't handle the song's lower, sultrier notes. Jackwash was right. Luella should have been singing instead.

Meanwhile, she was out of sight again.

"Where is Luella?" he shouted at Jackwash.

"The butterfly?" he snorted. "You want to catch her, you gonna need a net."

"You got that right." Willie finished his drink but held on to the glass. They were nowhere near a table, and he couldn't figure out where to put the empty. A man dressed in a gray suit and white Fedora glad-handed Jackwash, slurring something about the mud in Mexico. The way he said it made Willie think that he wasn't talking about dirt and water.

Jackwash pushed him away, laughing. "Go on, you old fool. I ain't here to do business," he said. The man stopped, swaying in place, then began to back away, apologizing. He stepped back into a couple trying to dance, and the dancing man slapped the Fedora off his head. The woman burst out laughing.

Luella skated by again, and Jackwash grabbed her by the arm. She frowned and tried to pull free, but he would have none of it. "Our old friend Willie Johnson is here to visit," he said. "Why don't you spend a minute saying hello."

"Hello," she said. She might as well have been talking to the police.

Willie kept his mouth shut.

"Well, that was nice." She pulled her arm free. "Now, I'm going to *dance*. You want to come with me?" She fluttered her eyelashes at Jackwash as she spoke.

"Wait a minute," he said. "Don't you have anything to say to your old friend?"

She turned to face Willie, fire in her eyes. "Well, now that you mention it, I sure do. Who do you think you are, running away without a word for *two damn years*? You don't think people wonder about you? Hope you're okay? Hope you're still alive? Or don't people's feelings mean anything to you, Willie Johnson?"

With her hands on her hips and her chin out like a boxer, he couldn't help but smile.

"What is so funny?" she demanded. Was it his imagination, or had her eyes gone darker still?

"I'm smiling because you're so damn cute," he said.

Jackwash frowned and started to say something but the sound of the warning buzzer interrupted him. The band stopped playing. Club employees moved through the crowd, collecting glasses. Luella wandered off again, so Jackwash grabbed Willie's empty glass and handed it to a passing busboy.

"What's going on?" Willie asked.

"Police. They raid every few months so's they look clean. Club manager is stalling them up front. All part of the show." He gave Willie a knowing glance. "Only time they ever *find* anything is when somebody forgets to pay for protection."

Once the room was clear, the band started up again. A half dozen uniformed officers began weaving their way through the room, sniffing glasses and stopping to chat with people they clearly knew.

"Like part of the floor show," Willie said. He paused for a moment, taking a deep breath. "So, tell me. What's with the marks on Luella's arm?"

Jackwash stared straight ahead for a moment and then turned. His face was stone. "Mind your business."

"Is heroin your business now?"

Jackwash looked away.

"You told me you'd stay clear of the tar."

"That what's botherin' you?"

Willie needed to shut up. He could see it in the way his friend's lips had pressed together and the way his muscles bunched up around his shoulders. But Willie was not so good at silence. "I don't give a damn about it if you don't. But you dragged Luella into your shit, didn't you?"

His answer came in a low growl. "Don't go dizzy over Luella. That's all I got to say."

"That ain't right, and you know it."

Jackwash stood, arms folded and mouth clamped shut.

"A man ought to take care of his woman."

"What do you know about it?" Jackwash's face twisted with anger. "You been alone all these years. What makes you an expert?"

"I know what's right and what's not. And so do you."

"Don't tell me what I know."

"I'll say whatever I want. We're family."

Jackwash nearly choked. "Family? White boy, has you got a mirror?"

"Don't," Willie said.

"Don't what?"

"Don't act like we haven't been best friends all your breathing life."

"Friends don't sniff around Luella like a dog trippin' on his tongue."

Jackwash knew. Once said out loud, the accusation couldn't be ignored. "I never touched her," he said.

Jackwash stared past Willie, his face suddenly blank again. "We done."

"Done." Willie stepped back and tilted his head, looking at his friend. He tried to smile. Part of him understood he was saying goodbye to his oldest friend, maybe forever. "I'll be seeing you." His voice came out in a croak.

"Abyssinia." Jackwash did not smile back.

CHAPTER TEN: MERCANTILE GOODS

"It's easier for a camel to pass through the eye of a needle than for a rich man to make a blues record."
~Hugh Laurie

1969
Fort Collins, Colorado
Both of them were up before dawn. Kennedy, who'd slept in the bed this time, woke feeling refreshed and ready for the day. Willie, who'd slept (or not) on the couch, was in the kitchen making breakfast. He had the window over the sink open. Kennedy could hear birds on the lawn, chirping the sun up. Willie had some eggs floating in bacon fat on the stove. A stack of toast slices sat on the table, next to a greasy napkin piled with bacon.

"Say, I forgot to tell you," Kennedy said. "I busted your cactus plant when I was cleaning yesterday."

"I noticed," Willie said. "No matter. I think the thing was dead anyway."

"At least half-dead."

"Yeah. Hard to tell with a cactus. You want your eggs flipped, or straight up?"

"Straight up, I guess."

"What time do you expect this Newport fella?"

"Lunchtime is what they said." Kennedy sighed. "Long time to wait."

Willie smiled. "Nah. Been waiting forty years. I can wait a few hours more."

"Which songs are you gonna play?"

"I guess I ought to play *Bitch Train*. That's what brought him here, right?" He scooped two fried eggs from the skillet onto Kennedy's plate, shoveling them with a spatula. Flakes of something black covered the eggs.

"What's this black stuff?" Kennedy asked.

"Scorch from the bacon," Willie said. "Don't worry. It tastes good."

"You should play *Sins in Blue,* too." Kennedy popped an egg yolk with a piece of toast. "That's a great song."

Willie grunted.

Kennedy took a bite. Eggs, basted in grease. Pretty good, really. "What's that mean? A grunt doesn't mean yes or no."

"That song isn't like the rest of my music," Willie said. "If he's expecting *Bitch Train*, a blues-jazz blend isn't going to impress him."

"Why did you name your song *Bitch Train* anyway?"

"I didn't." Willie sat down to his eggs, smashing them with a piece of toast, sopping up the yolk and bacon fat. "At first, I called the song *Misery Train*. I changed the words and the title the day I recorded it."

"Why?"

"Because I was drunk and angry, and that's the sort of thing I did back then." He chewed a little and swallowed. "I'm a milder sort, now. Even-tempered and all." He finished with a half-grin that made Kennedy laugh.

"Are you going to play the real song, or the version you recorded?"

"The version I recorded. Your eggs are getting cold."

"You're right. I don't want them to coagulate."

Willie laughed. "You're a funny kid. You know that?"

"Funny or funny looking?"

"Now that you mention it, your head is shaped wrong."

"I'm sorry I ever told you about that!" Kennedy sat back in mock exasperation. "My parents had terrible taste in names."

"What name would you have if the choice was yours?"

That one stumped him. Kennedy thought of people he'd known growing up. Travis Bunch was the quarterback at his high school. His first name was pretty cool—an athlete's name. Johnny was a guitarist's name—Johnny Winter. Johnny B. Goode. "I don't know," he said finally. "I never considered it, because I didn't have much choice in the matter."

Willie shook his head. "Name don't make the person. The person makes the name."

Kennedy thought and then laughed. "Bullshit. If your daddy named you Francis, you'd have never played guitar."

"I'd have played," Willie said. "Might have played church music instead of the blues, though."

"Francis Johnson, the man with one dick name."

Willie stood and headed for the sink. "Enough nonsense. We need to clean up these dishes."

Kennedy groaned. "You're all business." He glanced at the sink. "How many damned dishes did we get dirty?"

Willie turned on the tap to fill the sink.

"Can't I sit here a minute and let those eggs settle?"

"Work first. Play later."

"So says the man who avoided working for the first thirty years of his life."

Willie nodded, not looking back. "True. But I learned better along the way. That's something you'll have to figure out. It's not enough to work when you feel like it. You learn to work when you feel like crap. If you don't, you won't be able to work when you're my age, because you'll feel like crap every single day."

Kennedy considered mentioning Willie's drinking then but thought better of it. Instead, he asked, "So, what changed you?"

Willie glanced over his shoulder. "I'll answer as soon as you move your ass out of that chair." When Kennedy stood and grabbed plates from the table, Willie continued. "Easy answer would be the army. If your country goes to war and you enlist, you grow up mighty fast."

"Did you enlist after Pearl Harbor?"

"Nope. I waited three months, hoping we'd whip the Nazis and Japs right away. Didn't happen. I wasn't eating regular by then, so I signed the papers and off I went. Free meals and all."

"Why weren't you eating regular?"

"The music dried up."

"What do you mean?"

Willie stopped washing the dishes and turned around, leaning back against the sink. "If I'm going to talk, you're going to clean."

"I'm doing it," Kennedy said, taking dishes to the sink.

"Scrape them plates into the trash first." Willie shook his head. "Didn't do dishes at home, did you?"

"No. Mom did them."

"Man needs to know how to cook and how to do dishes and laundry. Otherwise, he'll get the idea that a woman's purpose is keeping house. You think that and you'll end up alone."

"You live alone," Kennedy grumbled. When he looked up, he saw pain in Willie's expression. "Hey, I'm sorry. I'm being a brat." Willie looked away. "What did you mean when you said the music dried up?"

"I overstayed my welcome," Willie said. "You can relate to that, can't you?" He cleared his throat. "After Prohibition, big-city nightclubs took the place of the jukes and membership clubs. The owners wanted their places to be as classy as the white folks' clubs, so they hired full bands and headliners. In the rougher neighborhoods, crime chased out the white patrons, and I wasn't welcome any more. Meanwhile, the white roadhouses and bars became a little less tolerant of the music I played." He closed his eyes and shook his head.

"What?"

"I'm remembering one place in particular. East Texas. I played about a song and a half, and some big bucket of peanuts starts hollering at me to stop playing *race music*. I had been drinking some—"

"No doubt."

"Am I gonna tell this story?"

Kennedy sat down.

"At any rate, I was less than polite. Next thing I know, I'm flat on my back, bleeding from the mouth, and that big son of a bitch had my guitar in his hands. He raised it up to smash it, and I called out to him to stop. I said, 'Don't do it. My friend give me that guitar.' He handed it over and said, 'All right, then. But get on out of here, trash.'"

Kennedy sat silent.

"I notice you stopped cleaning.'

Kennedy stood up. "Was that the same guitar that's in the living room?"

"Very same one," Willie said. "Held on to it ever since Jackwash gave it to me."

"I don't get it. Why didn't the guy smash it?"

"It was the Depression," Willie said. "Folks didn't have much, so they respected what little there was to go around."

"So, you couldn't play for white folks either?'

Willie gave him a rueful smile. "Some of it was my fault. I never did know how to keep my mouth shut. I said or did the wrong thing in enough places to keep myself generally unwelcome. By the time the war came around, I'd pretty much given music up for good."

"Then the army changed you?"

"After the war, I discovered that I worked harder than everyone around me. Caught me by surprise. I think sometimes I knew how to work all along—I was never shy about practicing the guitar. Anyway, I had no trouble finding work. I still couldn't hold on to a dollar, but I didn't worry about that."

"And you kept the guitar."

"My Aunt Beatrice kept it for me during the war. First night home, I wanted two things—a bottle and that guitar. She left me alone that night. Even let me drink. I was so grateful that I told her I'd say a prayer for her. She said . . ." He paused to laugh. "She said, 'That's fine, but I don't imagine the Lord takes much stock in the prayers of sinners.'" He met Kennedy's gaze. "And now here we are, and you know most of the story."

"What happened to Jackwash?" Kennedy asked. The question was out of his mouth before he could stop it.

"He died." Willie glanced at the kitchen clock. "This Newport fellow could be early. We need to move."

When the house had been properly tidied, Willie sat on the living room couch, waiting.

"This is the part I hate," Kennedy said.

"Get used to it," Willie said. "Adult life is made up of long periods of waiting, interrupted by short bursts of disaster." Kennedy nodded as if he understood exactly what Willie meant.

Noon came and went, and Willie began to show signs of impatience. He bounced his leg up and down as he sat, and let out a loud sigh every once in a while. At one o'clock, he asked, "Are you sure he was coming at noon?"

"He said *around lunchtime*."

"Did you give him the right address?"

"I did. I'm sure of it." Kennedy sat still for a moment, and then repeated the address out loud, adding, "That's right, isn't it?"

"Yup," Willie said.

Minutes dripped slow like molasses. The room was steaming, and Willie opened the door to cool things off—then shut it again to keep out the flies. "I been through this before," he muttered.

Kennedy sat, sulking. Did Willie think he made the visit up? That's what he'd think for sure if the man didn't show. *Where was he, anyway?*

"I been through this before," Willie repeated.

· · · · ·

1934

New Iberia, Louisiana

Alan Lomax and his father John had come to bayou country in hopes of recording authentic French-speaking Creole blacks. The music was unknown outside of the state, and for the two archivists, the prospect of uncovering new, unheard music was intoxicating.

John spent his days wherever they boarded, writing another book, so Alan did most of the recording. If he turned up anything special, John would return with his son and record more. The duo financed their project with book income, along with speaking fees and grant money. Their recording equipment, stored in their car, came from a

Rockefeller Foundation grant—including a 300-pound recording machine that cut aluminum discs, two 75-pound batteries, a vacuum tube amplifier, a mixing board, and a microphone. Whenever possible, Alan drove his roving studio right up to the home of the person he was recording, or to a sleepy nearby business with enough room to cut a disc.

The sight of Alan's rig often drew a crowd. While recording a local accordion player, a bystander approached Alan with a tale about the "greatest guitar player alive." The bystander was drunk, and other onlookers were quick to mention that he'd served time for manslaughter, which had the opposite of the expected effect. John took special interest in the man's opinion, as he believed that music should be studied from a social and cultural perspective. People on the margin of society carried special cachet with Alan Lomax.

"Man's name is Willie Johnson. You want a *real* recording, you needs to record Willie. I see'd him last night. I plays myself, but this man? Plays the blues like the devil crawled up behind him and helped out with an extra set of fingers."

Alan made arrangements to record this *bluesman extraordinaire* on the following day, with the help of the owner of the mercantile, who also provided certain supplies to a nearby juke. The juke's owner knew Willie, though he didn't think much of him.

Alan promised to meet Willie at noon, a commitment he couldn't keep. When he woke up that morning, he found his left passenger-side tire flat. His dad helped as best he could, unloading the equipment so they could jack up the car and put the bald spare on. By the time Alan was done sweating in the dirt, he was two hours late.

· · · · ·

Bullshit. Record a record, like a radio star? Some story.

Willie tapped on the store owner's counter. "You got something to drink back there?"

"You know I don't have nothin' like that. Prohibition." The owner had a mustache and beard, fine as frog's hair. His store was a little shabby—everything in Louisiana was shabby during the Depression—but not the man's facial hair. That was straight, white, and perfect.

Willie tapped again. "I'm in a bad mood. I walked here from Lydia, and it's hot out. I need a drink."

"How 'bout lemonade?"

"How 'bout I shove my guitar up your ass?"

"You'd do that to your guitar?"

"Might as well," Willie said. "It ain't doin' me no good today." He reached into his pocket and pulled out some coins. "In lieu of violence, I might be persuaded to pay you."

"Fair enough," the owner said, pulling a bottle from under the counter. During the exchange, he'd kept a straight face, but the creases at the corners of his eyes gave him away—he was enjoying himself. "Go ahead and drink from the bottle. This batch will kill any disease you're carrying."

Willie slapped his money on the counter, took a pull, and winced. "Damn!" he said. "This liquor makes a fine revenge on any man who threatens you."

"I wasn't worried, Willie Johnson. I heard you can't fight for shit."

"There's many a man that's beaten me down who'd agree with you."

"Women, too."

Willie laughed. "What's your name?"

"Melvin Guidry."

Willie held out his hand. "Willie Johnson."

Guidry shook his hand. "Pleased to make your acquaintance."

Willie took another drink. "Nice shop you have here."

Guidry glanced out of the dusty front window and shrugged. "As you can see, business is slow."

"You seem like a good ol' boy. I'd buy something off the shelf, but I think all my money's going to this liquor."

Guidry counted the coins and then looked at the bottle. "I'll tell you when you're done," he said.

The money ran out just as Alan Lomax arrived. By then, Willie was drunk.

Having spent years in jukes and after-hours clubs, he was no stranger to playing while intoxicated. Lomax, however, seemed nonplussed.

"You're Willie Johnson?" he asked. His thick eyebrows arched up on his forehead like two fat caterpillars. He pursed his lips and shook his head.

"What were you expecting?"

"A bluesman," Alan said.

"You don't record white men, is that it?" It was a straightforward question. Willie had been turned away because of his skin color before and took no offense beyond the wasted time.

"I record plenty of white musicians," Lomax said. "Recorded people all across Texas, among other places." He squinted. "But you're drunk."

"Won't matter," Willie said. "Set up. I'll play like you never heard before."

With Guidry's permission, Lomax backed his car right up to the front steps of the shop and staged his equipment. Willie grabbed a chair from the side of the porch and sat down to tune. The hot afternoon sun and the whiskey built up a powerful thirst, so he asked Guidry for a glass of cold water. Guidry brought him the aforementioned lemonade instead, and the sugar seemed to revive him.

After Lomax set the volume levels, Willie launched into *Rising, High-Water Blues*—a Blind Lemon song, but his throat still wasn't right, and his playing was unusually stiff. When the song was finished, it seemed like Lomax had finished, too. The recording was nothing special, especially the way Willie had played. Lomax reached for the microphone. Willie shooed him away. "You came to hear my guitar. That was a warmup. Now, I'm gonna let it rip." And he would, too, because he was hot and drunk and angry, and this man didn't seem to think he was any good.

"These aluminum discs are expensive," Lomax said. "I didn't know I was recording a warmup. You said you were ready to play." His lips were pursed up again, but he stepped back to his machine to ready himself for the second song. "What's this one called?"

"*Bitch Train*," Willie said.

Lomax frowned in apparent disgust, but he checked the dials and pointed at Willie.

And Willie played.

When the song was over, Lomax switched off his machine and stared at Willie, his hand propping his chin. After a while, he said, "Well, I'll give you this much. A man said yesterday that you played like the devil was lending a hand, and I guess he was right."

"So, am I gonna be on the radio?"

"What made you think that?"

"That's what they told me," Willie said, trying to hide his disappointment.

"No, sorry. I'm recording for archival purposes. Authentic folk music. And frankly, you don't fit in much with what I'm looking for."

"Why is that?"

"You're playing someone else's music."

"But I took the blues and made it my own," Willie said.

Lomax shook his head. "Wasn't yours to take."

CHAPTER ELEVEN: WILLIE'S PLACE

"Some of the greatest blues music is some of the darkest music you've ever heard."
~Bruce Springsteen

1969
Fort Collins, Colorado
"He's not coming," Willie said.

Kennedy stared at the clock. Three in the afternoon. "He said he'd be here, Willie. I swear, he—"

"I believe you." Willie sat with his hands on his knees, back erect. "It's all right. I didn't expect anything out of this business."

Kennedy winced. "He promised—"

"I know that, Kennedy. But people promise things all the time." Willie gave his head a slow shake. "And good things are mostly reserved for good people."

"What do you mean?"

Willie wouldn't meet his gaze. "I mean I've done too many bad things to get a break this late in the game." He sat back and coughed. The sound was wet with phlegm.

Kennedy stood up. "I'm gonna go to a pay phone and call George Wein."

"Sit down," Willie said. "We got everything we need here. I have a bottle in the kitchen cupboard and a leftover burrito in the refrigerator.

Drinks and appetizers. No bouncers. No lines at the bathroom. This might be the best bar in Fort Collins. *Willie's Place*."

Kennedy bit his lip at first, but when Willie stood and headed for the kitchen, he blurted, "Don't do it."

Willie stopped and turned, surprised.

"It would be like history repeating itself."

Willie stared at him for a moment and returned to the couch. "So, we wait?"

"We wait."

Willie returned to the couch, slumped forward, his arms dangling between his legs. Kennedy paced the room, pausing to look out the window with every circuit, as if by looking, he could make the man materialize on the lawn.

Willie sighed. "It was fun to think about," he said. "Playing again? For a crowd of people who like the blues? Fine dream."

"It may still happen."

"I don't think so."

"You're just trying to talk yourself down, so you won't be disappointed. And you shouldn't. You need to stay ready. He may still show up. Like Lomax."

"And look how well that turned out," Willie said, practically spitting the words. He wiped his mouth with his shirtsleeve. "Like I said, I didn't really expect anything out of this."

"What have we been doing for the last few days, then?"

"Drinking and talking over old times. And pretending." He paused. "It's like playing the numbers. Everybody's got the winning ticket, right up until the winner is announced. Everybody has plans for the money they'll never get to spend. They know what car they're gonna buy. They pay off their momma's debts. They'll even put something aside—"

"He's here."

"What?"

Kennedy walked to the door and pulled it open, calling, "You looking for Willie Johnson? He's in here."

The man stood halfway between the sidewalk and the front door. "I'm late," he said.

Kennedy smiled. "Glad to see you."

The man was not wearing a suit, as Kennedy had expected. Instead, he wore shorts, sandals, and a tie-dye tee shirt with the slogan *Paix au Vietnam* in block letters across the front. His silver Chrysler sat at the curb behind him.

"Come on in," Kennedy said, stepping aside to allow him entry. Willie sat on the couch, seemingly frozen.

"Howard Warden," the man said, extending a hand to Kennedy.

"Kennedy Barnes. And this is Willie."

Warden turned.

Willie stood, hobbled over to his guitar and picked it up. Kennedy had put a stool in the corner for him. He sat down and began strumming.

"Have a seat," Kennedy said.

Warden stood still.

Willie played the opening chords of *Bitch Train*. His voice sounded scratchier than usual. Kennedy wished he'd stop singing and start playing, and as if reading his mind, Willie began picking, and the flurry of single notes filled the room. How could the old man's fingers move so fast? He raced over minor chord arpeggios, sliding up the guitar neck, finger-dancing to the thump of the base string.

And then he stopped and looked up.

"Well," Warden said. "Well, well."

"And he's been doing that for thirty-five years," Kennedy gushed. "Long before anyone thought of playing like that. Willie Johnson . . .invented rock and roll."

Willie grimaced. "I've explained to the boy that there were plenty of others playing that sort of—"

"Ike Turner, for one," Warden said.

"Willie recorded for Alan Lomax twenty years before *Rocket 88*."

"Seventeen years," Willie said.

"Well," Warden repeated. His forehead wrinkled, and his upper lip twitched. Was Warden just tired, or didn't he like the music?

"Play another song," Kennedy said. Warden hadn't sat down yet. If Willie didn't play something *right now*, the man might leave.

"Here's one of mine," Willie said. He pulled his knife from his pocket and began to play, using the knife as a slide. The notes buzzed and whined. This time, Willie's voice seemed stronger as he crooned the lyrics.

When you're talkin' women, you're talkin' money, too.
You just can't avoid it, can't separate the two.

Don't matter what your heart says, you're broke down to the bone.
Them pretty womens leave you there standin' all alone.

Just give me wine and wicked women.
That is all I crave.
Wine and wicked women,
'till I'm in my grave.

Kennedy hadn't heard Willie's slide work before. He stood, openmouthed. The knife made a scratchy, metallic sound as it slid up and down the strings. When the song was over, Kennedy chanced another look at Warden. His expression had softened a little.

"Nice," Warden said.

"What's the verdict?" Willie asked.

The furrows returned to Warden's forehead. "You play very well."

"He'll be a hit at your festival," Kennedy said.

Warden shook his head. "I came out here—and I have to say, I drove quite a bit out of my way—to listen to an old bluesman."

"I play the blues," Willie said. He had an odd look on his face—part amusement and part anger. His fingers had closed around the knife, gripping it tight.

"There's a difference between a white man who plays the blues and a bluesman," Warden said. His voice had a finality to it. "The Newport Folk Festival is dedicated to introducing authentic American music. Music that's been lost, and now found. I'll be candid with you gentlemen. I came here expecting to hear a black musician—"

"I never said he was black!" Kennedy said.

"A lie by omission." Warden's expression had become grimmer still. "I am trying not to take my frustration out on you, Mr. Johnson. You clearly have skills. But I've been sent on a goose chase, and it's difficult not to feel somewhat used in this situation. As I said, we feature *authentic* music at the festival."

"I played jukes and clubs all over the south. I played for tips or drinks and a hot meal. I slept in boxcars and rode the rails from town to town. I drank bootleg liquor and got my ass kicked by black and white men alike. I loved and lost, and the whole time, I played the blues. I *lived* the blues."

"And in your travels, did you encounter black musicians who played the blues from the heart, yet never had a chance, simply because of the color of their skin? Shouldn't they get a chance, too? Aren't those the artists I should be seeking out?"

Willie set his guitar aside.

"As I said, you play well. But we showcase genuine artists who never had a chance to play, to an audience that's never heard the true voice of a downtrodden people. That's a sacred trust—one that I will not abandon."

Willie nodded. "Well, the blues can rest easy, knowing you're watchdogging."

Warden stepped back. "You gentlemen wasted my time, not the other way around." He opened the door and turned for a last word. "In the end, it's a matter of respect. Respect for someone else's music."

"Actions, not words," Willie said. "You respect something—love something—you make it a part of your life. You don't stick it in a museum, under glass, so's it won't get away. You think you're *protecting* something? All you're doing is charging admission."

"I'm done here," Warden said.

When the door slammed, Kennedy slumped back against the wall, near tears. "I can't believe—"

"I can," Willie said. "This ain't the first time I've had this conversation. Seems like there's always someone ready to decide who can do what, and who can't." He stood and stretched, shaking his arms. "Damn. I'm half-glad that's over."

Kennedy stared.

"*I told you*. I didn't expect much. I know how the world works. Everybody's all worried about prejudice these days, talking about ought to do this, and ought to do that. It's all a bunch of words. The same fools are in charge, telling people what to do and what *not* to do." He walked into the kitchen and returned with a bottle of whiskey and two glasses. "Nothing holding us back, now. *Willie's Place* is open for business. Best prices in town. Free." He poured two shots and started to hand one to Kennedy, pulling back at the last moment. "You got an I.D.?"

"Willie . . ."

He shoved the drink in Kennedy's hand and took a sip of his own. "No sweat, kid. You did your best. And I don't deserve any better."

"Why do you say that? You're a great guitarist and a great man. You treat me better than my own family—"

"Speaking of that . . . have you called your mother yet?"

Kennedy blushed and turned away.

Willie finished his drink and poured another. "Don't you think she deserves better than that? And your father? You may have your problems with him, but don't you think he worries?"

"He broke my records."

"Now you sound like a little kid."

Kennedy swallowed the drink, nearly choking. "Give me the bottle," he croaked.

"Go easy. This is my only bottle, and it's got to last the night."

Kennedy poured a shot into the glass and took it to the couch. "What now?"

Willie downed his drink. "Same as last week. I work."

"Why don't you retire?"

"I'm old enough," Willie said. "But I don't have two dollars to rub together."

"They pay Social Security, don't they?"

"I worked off the books most of my life," Willie answered. "I'm a musician, remember? I could get something, all right, but it wouldn't cover rent. I'm going to have to keep working."

"What happens when you can't work anymore?"

Willie didn't answer.

"Jesus," Kennedy said. "What a mess. Why couldn't they just give us a chance?"

"Don't deserve one," Willie said.

"Why do you keep saying that? What did you ever do that was so awful?" He'd asked the question again, and he hadn't meant to—not really. Not now, anyway. He sat staring at the drink in his hand. The room was hot, and the taste of the liquor made him sick to his stomach. Flies buzzed in the window behind him.

Willie crossed over and sat back down on the stool next to his guitar. He poured himself another glass—a full one this time—and coughed. He took a sip, and coughed again, hacking up something from the back of his throat. "I saw Luella one more time," he said. Then he was silent. The minutes stretched past, but Kennedy didn't prod him. The old man would either tell his story or he wouldn't. Either way, it was his story to tell.

· · · · ·

1936

Cruger, Mississippi

The town had changed since Willie'd been on the road. He'd walked from the train station over the bridge, his guitar slung over his back like a rifle, past the graveyard with its odd brick plots and headstones, like tiny coffin-shaped kilns. The doors to Mr. Green's drug store were still open, though maybe not for long. The town was shrinking, drying up and blowing away. The church where Willie and Jackwash had gone as children stood upright, but the parched wood looked one match shy of a bonfire.

Aunt Beatrice was much the same as the town—older and more withered. She'd either lost some of her faith or her desire to club him over the head with it. She even let him play guitar in his room and didn't badger him to find work until the third day.

News of Jackwash's death came from a cousin who'd heard what happened from another cousin. "They shot him three times," he told

Willie. "Two in the head, and one in his pecker. Somebody was makin' a *statement.*"

Who had he crossed? Willie would never know. He asked around about the body, but nobody knew anything. If there'd been a way to get him home, Willie'd have seen to Jackwash's burial himself. "They probably ran him through the grinder," the cousin said. "Might come across him if'n you buy some o' that Chicago-made sausage." Since moving north, Jackwash had never looked back, and the folks back home weren't inclined to remember him kindly.

Home, flat broke, and run out of most of the jukes and clubs he once played, Willie had time to grieve. Passing a field where they'd played catch with a ball Jackwash made out of packing tape, or stopping in the Bakery & Meat Market, where Jackwash stole a string of hot dogs while Willie made a distraction out of selecting a loaf of bread he had no money for, Willie greeted each marker from the past as a fresh regret.

He didn't ask about Luella, so she'd been home for a month before he learned she was back. He waited another week before going to see her.

Luella's mother lived a quarter mile from the church. The wood shack was raised up a foot and a half on log posts in case of flood, or perhaps to give the dog a cool place to wait out the hot summer sun. Over the years, the floor had sagged, bowing down almost to the ground in some places. The roof had stayed tall around the stovepipe, but the rest was sinking in like the floor. When Willie came to pay a call, Luella and her mother sat sweating on the porch. Luella said something, and her mother scurried inside, shutting the door behind her.

Willie stopped some distance from the porch, not saying anything.

"Is that you, Willie Johnson?"

"You know it is."

"You a little thinner than the man I used to cook for."

"You got no room to talk." Luella wore a housedress that did little to hide her wasted frame. Her arms were matchsticks. The closer he got, the worse they looked—scarred and riddled with abscesses. Her skin had a yellow tint, or was that just the sun? She smiled, and he could see that her gums had receded.

"You heard about Jackwash?"

Willie nodded. "Where's he buried?"

"Don't know and don't care," she said. "When he died, he left me without a damned cent of my own. Had to come back home *on my own*." She leaned forward. "Do you know what it's like for a woman alone on the road?"

"No, I don't."

"Well, you can imagine, can't you?" Her eyes were red and wet.

"Who killed him?"

"That's the question, ain't it? He knew everybody in that town, and they knew him, so there was plenty of people with good reason to kill him. He was a bad man."

"He was my friend."

"He didn't have *nothin'* nice to say about you."

Willie looked away. This wasn't the woman he remembered.

"I'm surprised to see you come around," she said. "I been home for weeks."

"I just heard about it."

Her gaze drilled into him like the sun overhead. "When they told me Jackwash was dead, I thought to myself, well, that Willie Johnson will show up now. He'll come save ol' Luella and take her away from this damned place. I *waited* for you to come."

"How was I supposed to know that?" Willie said. "I seen you once in four years, and you were none too happy to see me that one time."

"I was happy," she said. She sat back, her head against the stained wood behind her. She patted her hair and wiped her mouth with the back of her hand. "But I was with Jackwash, and he was a jealous man . . ." She closed her eyes, a wistful look crossing her face. "He didn't want *nobody* to talk to me. Kept me under lock and key."

"You looked pretty free to me." He remembered watching her flit from place to place in the club, smiling and laughing. She'd been so beautiful, and for what?

"I didn't have nothin' to my name. Not a dime."

"Maybe he didn't want you to waste it on junk."

In the silence, Willie heard the drone of insects. He listened for birdsongs, but there were none.

"That much is probably true," she said. "So, you gonna stand there, or come up here and sit by me?"

"I'm fine where I am," Willie said. His head swam in the heat. He'd loved her—he loved her still—and this was how she ended up? She had his heart in her hands. Instead, she chose Jackwash, and needles, and ended up in a shack with newspaper pasted over broken shingles. She could have been with him.

He closed his eyes. And what would that have gotten her? Holed up in a corner room at Aunt Beatrice's, talking about broken dreams and trying to earn a living in a country dying around them. He clenched his fists until his fingernails cut into his palms.

"You still play?"

He nodded. He was too upset to speak.

She swallowed. "I still sing."

He didn't answer.

"I was thinkin' you and I could get together. I could sing, and you could play guitar. We could make some money—"

His laugh interrupted her. "Yeah, because folks will be glad to spend their last dime to see a white boy and a colored junkie play the blues."

His words struck her like a fist, and she shuddered. "I just thought . . ."

Willie waited.

She swallowed, and it looked like it hurt her to do so. "Come in out of the sun, Willie."

"I don't think so." He would rather stand there, stewing in his own sweat, than step on that porch.

"There was a time," she said, speaking slowly as if weighing her words, "when you seemed to like me a little. Like you might want to be with me. Remember when you were sick? I took care of you, and we used to talk a lot. We talked 'bout *everything*. I miss that. I really do. Seemed like you liked that, too, didn't you?"

She looked so frail and so old. How could she have let this happen to herself?

She patted her hair again. "I guess I've changed. I'm not so pretty as I once was."

The anger bubbled over, and he spoke without thinking. "No, you don't look the same. Fact is, looking at you now, seein' how spent you are, I can't believe you were *ever* beautiful."

She bowed her head. She might have been crying, given the way her shoulders trembled, but she wouldn't look up, so he couldn't be sure. He waited a moment before turning away.

On the way home, he thought of all the things he'd done in his life. He'd used his knife in anger. Drank himself into a stupor. Stolen a time or two. Danced with the devil more than once. But none of that had bothered him. This, though, was different. The weight of the sin he'd just committed pressed down on him and made him sick.

He could go back and apologize. But he kept on walking, one foot in front of the other. When he reached Beatrice's, he grabbed his guitar and headed out of town. By midnight, he was in a boxcar, moving north.

• • • • •

1969
Fort Collins, Colorado

"Two days later, I turned around," Willie told Kennedy. "Caught a southbound freight and rode it straight back. Jumped the train in the middle of the night, with nobody to thumb a ride from. Walked eight miles in the dark. Got there as the sun was coming up on the third day. I had it in my head to make things right, but it was too late. She was already buried." He paused to finish another glass of whiskey. In the time that it took to tell his tale, he'd finished half a bottle. When he spoke again, he slurred. "She hung herself."

Kennedy said, "You don't know."

"Don't know what?"

"Don't know if she killed herself because of you. She might have done it anyway."

Willie closed his eyes. "You're wrong. I *know*." He reached behind him, fumbling for his guitar, nearly knocking it over. Leaning out, he almost fell off the stool. "That's what the song is about," he said. "It's about killing the only woman I ever loved. Killing her, just the same as if I put my knife to her throat." He started to play *Sins in Blue* again, but he'd had too much to drink, and he couldn't finger the chords. He stopped, started over, and then stopped again.

"You don't have to play that," Kennedy said.

"Yes, I do. I need to play this song *now*, play it for her." He tried again, and fumbled again, dropping his pick. When he reached down to grab it, he tumbled off the stool, knocking the whiskey bottle over in the process.

"God damn you," Willie said to himself.

"Just let it go."

"Might as well," Willie said, struggling to his feet. "Been playing the blues my whole life, and all I got to show for it is a guitar give to me by a dead friend, and a song I can't play about a dead woman. Fuck."

"Stop it, Willie."

"Stop it yourself." Willie grabbed the guitar by the neck and swung it around, smashing it on the floor, snapping it in two. The body, still attached by the strings, hung from the neck in his hands. He seemed surprised. "Well," he said. "That's that."

CHAPTER TWELVE: THE N&R BAR

"Audiences like their blues singers to be miserable."
~Janis Joplin

1969
Fort Collins, Colorado
Kennedy fed quarters into the pay phone and waited for the operator to make the connection. He'd hoped his mother would answer, but of course, it was his father's voice that he heard—hard as hickory—saying, "Hello?"

"It's me." Pause. "Kennedy."

Silence. Then, "Are you all right?"

"Yes. I'm calling to say so."

"Where are you?"

"Fort Collins, Colorado."

"Colorado? Out west Colorado?"

If he'd been talking to Willie, he'd have said something smart like, "No, Colorado, Maine." But this was no time for sarcasm. "Yes, out West."

"What the hell . . ." His father's voice trailed off.

"I came out here to try to work out a music deal with an old musician I discovered. The deal fell through. Anyway, I'd been thinking about that instead of calling."

"Does this have something to do with that race music you listen to?"

"Willie is a white man." Kennedy knew he was prevaricating, but it seemed fitting that Willie's skin color—never much a benefit to himself—save Kennedy some difficult explanations.

"Willie who?"

"Willie Johnson."

"Sounds like a colored man . . ."

"In more ways than one," Kennedy said. The joke was out before he could stop it. He leaned into the pay phone booth, whacking his head on the frame.

"What was that?" his father demanded.

"I whacked my head," Kennedy said.

"Well, be careful." Pause. "Do you have any money?"

"Some."

"If I cable you some money, will you come home?"

"I'm coming home either way," Kennedy said. "If you'll have me."

"Do you have any idea what you put your mother through?" His father's voice rose, colored by that sharp edge that never failed to grate on Kennedy. "Do you know what this little adventure of yours cost her?"

Kennedy counted to five before answering. "That's something I can't undo. But I'll try and make it up to her as best I can."

When his father spoke again, the edge was gone. "Call me back in ten minutes. I have to figure out where you can pick up money."

Kennedy mumbled his goodbye and hung up.

Standing outside of the grocery, he glanced at the 24-hour burger joint across the street. The building looked like a glass cube wearing a stucco hat. The day was cooler than it would be come afternoon, and Kennedy's stomach rumbled. He didn't need to save *all* of his cash. A burger or fried chicken for breakfast sounded wonderful. He made his way across the street and to the front door, but the closer he got, the more overpowering the smell of grease became. By the time he reached the threshold, he'd changed his mind.

A big black bird perched on the crosswalk sign behind him seemed to regard, then dismiss him with a single caw.

What time was it? Was he really up this early? Back home, he never missed an opportunity to sleep in on the weekend. Behind the burger place, a young man hosed the pavement, cleaning in preparation for the day's business. Seemed like it would be fun to work in fast food. Did employees eat free? In a college town, a lot of cute girls came in to buy lunch. The work couldn't be too hard. He could put some money aside. Not for college, though. No way he was going to spend thousands of dollars on a piece of paper. If he wanted paper, he could unroll some in the bathroom.

What was he going to do, then?

Do what you love.

Can't make any money at that.

The first voice was Willie's. The answering voice was his father's. *Where's my voice?* he wondered. *What do I want to do?*

He knew the answer. Knowing *where* he wanted was the hard part. That being decided, he would have plenty of time to figure out the rest.

Back at the pay phone, his father explained where to pick up the cash he would wire. The stern-edged voice had returned. His father was, after all, a no-nonsense sort of man. Kennedy waited until the instructions had finished and said, "Got it."

"Well, then. Hurry home. And keep us posted."

Kennedy hesitated. He had something more to say, but his mouth was suddenly dry. "Umm."

"What?" Impatient now.

"I'm sorry. Sorry I didn't call. Sorry things got out of hand between us."

For a moment, Kennedy wondered if his father would apologize for breaking his records. Or punching him in the eye. His father's voice had gone husky. "You and I will be fine. Just make sure you make amends with your mother."

"Can I talk to her?"

"Yes. She's been waiting her turn."

· · · · ·

Willie slept through the alarm clock. His head ached, and his knees were swollen. He struggled to the bathroom, bouncing off the door frame because he couldn't walk straight. He was halfway through his morning piss when he remembered the guitar. The pang of sorrow that followed was real. He'd loved that damned thing. A fitting end, though. World's worst bluesman, shunned by blacks and whites alike, puts an exclamation point on a pointless career. *Good thing I still have my day job.*

Kennedy was nowhere to be found. Perhaps he was headed home. Good. The boy needed to mend fences before it was too late. Before leaving, he'd cleaned up the mess Willie had made of the living room, perhaps in place of a goodbye note. The guitar pieces were bagged, sitting on the kitchen table. That was good, too. Willie was loath to part with the thing, even in pieces, being that it was all he had left of Jackwash and Luella.

The walk to work just about spent him. His hip was on fire, and his kidneys hurt. He'd been drinking too much, and if he was going to survive another workweek, he was going to have to stop. The morning sun was already hot. Sweat soaked the neckline of his shirt and trickled down the small of his back—the price he paid for waking up late.

On that subject, he wondered if he still had his day job after all. Seemed like Mrs. C had been looking for a reason to fire him for months. By being late, he might just be handing her a good reason on a platter.

He hadn't yet punched his timecard when she poked her round face through the office door and called him in. "I need to talk to you." She wore enough makeup to mask any emotion, so he wasn't sure what to expect.

Her office was tiny, which only emphasized how large the woman was. She wore a white institutional uniform, better suited to a nurse. Her lips were crimson, and cobalt blue shadow ringed her eyes. She tapped her manicured nails on the desk. "I'm pretty annoyed with you."

Willie sniffed. The office smelled of the worst perfume he could imagine.

"Sorry I'm late—"

She interrupted. "Your little friend didn't show up yesterday."

Willie frowned.

"Rodney. Your little trainee. He didn't bother to come to work. He called in just before I was leaving for the day with some cock-and-bull story about feeling sick. I fired him." She sat back and exhaled. "The little shit called me a bitch!"

Willie nodded, trying to hide a smile.

"Anyway, everyone pitched in to help, but the laundry is a mess." She narrowed her blue eyes and leaned as far forward as her huge frame and tiny desk would allow. "I would have called you in to work, but *you don't have a phone.*"

"Yes, ma'am. I've been meaning to get one, but money only goes so far."

"Oh, don't tell me that. You have plenty of money. You make almost two bucks an hour." She shook her head. "You need to get a phone. It's the twentieth century. People need to be able to get ahold of you."

"That kid wasn't going to work out anyway."

"I *know*. All he did was flap his lips about how hard he worked, but on your days off, *nothing* got done." She sat back and wiped sweat from her forehead. "It's hot in here. You'd better get to work. There's a lot of laundry waiting for you, and the girls wiped out the clean sheets and towels an hour ago. Why are you late, by the way?"

"Had family in town. Had to see him off."

"Well," Mrs. C said, making a show of tidying a pile of papers. "You shouldn't let your personal life interfere with your career. A man your age should know that." Willie spent a frantic hour loading laundry in the big machines and folding what clean linen was ready for use. Then, while moving the laundry from maid to maid upstairs, Willie's hip buckled, and he went down hard. His knee was already swollen, and he would surely need a taxi to get to work the next morning.

But he wouldn't call in. He didn't want Mrs. C questioning his health.

As the day wore on, Willie had multiple opportunities to bemoan the liquor he'd had the previous evening. No matter. Halfway home from a ten-hour shift, he stopped for a beer at the N&R, a tiny bar next to the hotel on Walnut. Something to take the edge off a whiskey hangover that simply would not go away.

As he sat in the dark, the radio played *Honky Tonk Women* by the Rolling Stones. He'd heard that the Stones would be coming to Fort Collins that fall, playing in the new college gym. He closed his eyes and listened. The drummer hammered on a cowbell like his life depended on it. Crazy damned song.

The bar was nearly empty. Acquiring a liquor license hadn't been the boon the owners might have imagined, and Willie wondered about tiny neighborhood places like the N&R. Newer, bigger establishments were opening every day. The world was changing fast. Things Willie loved were sure to go away. They always did.

What would happen when he couldn't work anymore? How would he live? Glancing around the empty bar, Willie decided that there was no use thinking about it. The time to think about the future had passed thirty years earlier. When his body gave out, he'd be done. What would happen would happen.

But it wouldn't happen for a while. He still had some vinegar in his veins.

After he left, the beer sat sour in the pit of his stomach. He considered calling for that taxi, but it seemed like a waste to save just half a walk home with a full taxi fare.

Crossing campus, the students were absent for the evening, back in their dorms or out to parties. A few lonely stragglers studied in the grass or near the flower beds, but the loudest sound Willie could hear was his own labored breathing.

By the time he arrived home, he was ready to collapse. The front door opened as he reached for the knob, and Kennedy stepped out. They stared at each other for a few moments before Willie said, "I thought you went home."

Kennedy backed inside. "You look like you need to sit down."

"I do," Willie said. "I took a fall at work, and the knee and hip aren't cooperating."

"You're right about my leaving. I wanted to say goodbye first."

Willie moved past him, a hand on his shoulder for support, and dropped onto the couch, groaning. "Don't get old," he advised. "It's a constant source of disappointment." Kennedy's duffel bag sat near the door, ready for his exit. "You have enough money to get home?"

Kennedy nodded. "I had some left. And when I called my dad, he wired me more so I could take a bus."

"When's the bus leave?"

"I'm gonna hitch instead. I have a lot of thinking to do, and you can't think on a bus. Too much noise."

Willie nodded. "I've always preferred an open boxcar to a bus, myself. So, what's next?"

"I'll go out Highway 14 and—"

"I mean, what are you going to do when you get home?"

Kennedy blinked. "I'm hoping to get a job. Spend some time with my little brother, Jackson. Patch things up with my folks."

"College then?"

"No," Kennedy said. His voice was firm and certain. "Music."

"You don't play."

"And I never will. Not like you. But there are DJs and promoters and recording studios . . . and I know what I like."

"What's that?"

"*Authentic music.* Not like that man said yesterday. I mean real music. Honest. From the heart. Maybe I'll promote it. Maybe I'll spin wax. It doesn't matter. Music is going to be my life."

Willie snorted. "Won't that piss off your folks?"

Kennedy flashed the hint of a smile. "I'm already in the doghouse."

"Might go easier for you if you go ahead and buy that bus ticket."

"I had other use for the money." Kennedy pointed to the corner of the room.

Willie turned and saw a cream-colored electric guitar propped where his old acoustic used to sit, plugged into a small amplifier the size of a bread box. "What the hell did you do?" Willie asked.

"You'll get used to an electric really fast," Kennedy said. "The things you do will sound even better, once you get used to the feel."

"You shouldn't have done that."

"I had to. I'm the reason you smashed your guitar."

Willie turned back, frowning. "Nonsense. I was drunk and feeling sorry for myself."

"I failed us. I wanted to go to Newport—"

"You gave it your shot. Nothing to be ashamed of."

"Then, I pushed you. I shouldn't have done that."

Willie waited.

"I wanted to know what you'd done . . . who you'd killed. I made you tell the story, and then you smashed your guitar."

Willie licked his lips. "Kennedy. It wasn't you pouring that liquor down my throat. It wasn't you that had sins to confess. I broke that guitar *all on my own*."

"You believe that?"

"With all my heart," Willie said.

"I think you're lying to make me feel better."

"I don't lie," Willie said.

Kennedy stepped forward. "Well, I'm glad to hear it. Because it wasn't you who put junk in Luella's veins. And it wasn't you put a noose around her neck."

Willie started to speak, anger in his eyes, but stopped. He sat without speaking for a long while. "I think," he said at last, "that you just set me up, you little shit."

"Maybe. I'll admit I gave that speech some thought."

"You know I did her wrong, don't you? Luella?"

"You were cruel," Kennedy agreed. "But she killed herself. You can call yourself an accomplice, but you've already served time."

Willie stared straight ahead, a hard, vacant look in his eyes. "You're a good kid, Kennedy. I'm glad you set things right with your folks." He turned to gaze at the guitar again. "That is an ugly color."

"That's the only reason I got a good price. Probably sat in the pawnshop window so long, it drove away business. He was glad to cut me a deal. You going to play it for me?"

"No. I'll pick it up when you're gone. I'll send you a tape after I've had some time to figure it out." He turned back. "You're hitting the road, then?"

"I am."

"You have food? There's still some burrito in the fridge."

Kennedy laughed. "No, thanks."

Willie stood up, which took longer than it should have, and ambled across the room. He put his arms around Kennedy, saying, "I'm going to miss your big ol' misshapen head."

"And I'm gonna miss your grouchy, old man self."

Willie stepped back. "Thank you. For the guitar. For everything. You are a fine young man."

Kennedy smiled. He was clearly fighting tears again. "Only way to replace a guitar given to you by a friend is for a friend to give you another guitar. Or something like that."

"You keep in touch," Willie said. "You have the address. Write me a letter every once in a while."

"I will," Kennedy said. He picked up his duffel bag and opened the door, pausing as if to say more, blinking through his round glasses, but words wouldn't come, so he finally headed toward the sidewalk.

· · · · ·

Dear Willie,

Hope you are doing well. I am fine. I'm back home and working in a pizza shop. I toss dough in front of a window, so customers waiting can enjoy the show. I hate the smell of yeast like I think you must hate dirty towels.

I'm also a DJ for a pirate radio station here in the neighborhood. All the kids at the high school listen. I play mostly rock, though I slip in some blues whenever I can. I sold an ad to the local grocery store—our first paid ad—so Henry (who put the equipment together) lets me pretty much play anything I want.

And, I've been at the library, reading up on recording studios. There's a lot to learn.

It was good to see my little brother again. He's growing up fast. He likes football, which scares my mom. I've been practicing with him in the backyard. He's only seven, so I go easy on him.

I get along with my folks most of the time. My dad tries to be a good man, though we've had a lot of arguments about college. I've learned that it's easier to stay calm because he can't force me to do anything I don't want to do. Going to Colorado changed all that. When things get hot, I just shut up, and that goes a long way toward calming things down.

Of course, I don't always help matters. A week or two ago, the police brought me home from a bar. I had a fake I.D., but I guess it didn't look all that real. And Mom is still mad at me over the neighbor girl, Jenny. I'll have to tell you about that sometime, but I'm not putting it in writing.

Anyway, I hope you're well and enjoying the electric guitar. Don't give it up. If you ever quit the blues, it will be the death of you.

Your friend, Kennedy

• • • • •

1969

Fort Collins, Colorado

Willie took no time at all to get comfortable with the new guitar. The neck was maple wood—fast—with a slight curve to the fretboard, which was kind to his old fingers. He found that he could do everything he'd ever done on the acoustic and more. He taught himself some trills that made his lead work sound great. After a month, he got the idea to play to an audience again.

He talked the owner of the Town Pump into letting him play a short set at the bar. The bearded bluegrass player had an affection for old music and old musicians, and Willie fit both ends of that bill. On a Tuesday night, Willie set up his amp and guitar in the corner of the bar and began playing without any introduction. No more than three or four tables had a clear line of sight to him, hunched down as he was. His voice was scratchier than usual, and he thought he might scare them off, but the kids didn't seem to mind.

Willie played a few blues standards to open before playing some of his own music. He gave a thought to playing *Sins in Blue,* but he didn't think he could get through the song without weeping, so he played a Beatles tune instead.

At first, he was distracted by a dozen details, from the smell of smoke and alcohol to the way the pink neon reflected in one young blond girl's hair. But after a while, the bar seemed to slip away, and there was only the music—his music.

When he was done, he bent to unhook his little amp and slip his guitar into its canvas case. The blond college girl came up, hands folded in front of her black skirt and Jimi Hendrix tee shirt. "Mr. Johnson? I just wanted to tell you how much I enjoyed your music." He thanked her, and gave her his best sweet-old-man smile. The girl had nice legs.

Willie considered playing again some time, though the cab ride to and from home with his equipment was a little too pricey for his budget. But playing for a crowd again had been fun.

· · · · ·

As the weeks passed, he fumbled through his workweek in physical pain. His hip and knee were at war with his body. His congested lungs made it hard to breathe. Worse still was a mental state of constant regret. Telling his story to Kennedy was supposed to have been cathartic, but it hadn't eased the remorse or given him the measure of peace he'd longed for.

In the fall, Willie bought a ticket to see the Rolling Stones. He realized he'd never really attended a concert before. He *played* in them, but never sat through one as a fan. He recalled listening to the Stones and their cowbell at the N&R. They sounded okay. But when the radio announced the warmup acts, Willie pulled money from his savings for the ticket.

The concert was held at Moby Gym, just a short walk from Willie's home. Named for its odd whale shape, the gymnasium was the home of Colorado State University basketball. The facility could hold thousands of people in the stands and on the floor, and on that November night, the place was packed to capacity. Willie had a seat on the right-side bleachers, close enough to see everything on the stage below. When the music started, the wall of amplifiers hammered his ears. Oh, the things he could have done with equipment like that!

The first opening act was Lee Michaels, who had a pop hit with the song *Do You Know What I Mean?* Willie watched the set and applauded, but the kid wasn't who he'd braved the crowd to see.

When the second act came onstage, Willie was all ears. He'd never seen the immortal B.B. King perform live, and the man was here, in the Colorado mountains of all places, playing in a venue packed with white children.

King was decked out in a sparkling tux, his guitar *Lucille* riding his belly like a surfboard on a wave. He played his biggest hits, popping his notes, adding his signature finger tremolo, head rocked back and sweating under the spotlights. The crowd loved him.

Willie watched, half in wonder and half in envy. How had this come to be? A bluesman in Fort Collins? It was a brave new world, for sure.

Sandwiched by the crowd, Willie tried to focus on the stage, but distractions were everywhere. To his right, a young lady spent the night motionless, with her head between her knees. Beyond her, a young couple divided their time between watching the stage and watching the motionless girl. The boy looked worried, and the girl shook her head in disgust. The object of their attention looked dead.

When King played his biggest hit, *The Thrill is Gone*, the crowd went crazy. Some sang along. *They actually know the words.* Willie shook his head in amazement. Where did these kids learn about the blues?

After a short break, the Stones came on stage—skinny, shaggy boys sounding like they'd been raised up on Chuck Berry records. The crowd was noisy at first, making it hard for Willie to pay attention. When the band settled into music from their new album, the crowd simmered down a little, and Willie leaned forward, intrigued. B.B. King had been a fine showman, but these boys were taking the music back to the deep south, back to the juke.

The lead singer had a little bit of Howlin' Wolf's growl to him. The opening to one of the new songs was familiar—gritty, dirty blues chords played to a shuffle beat that changed speeds as the song developed. The itch in Willie's fingers told him that he wanted to play along. When the band suddenly downshifted into a slow blues, Willie caught some of the lyrics—something about a stalker going after young girls. When the song kicked back into high gear again, the song returned to the shuffle that opened the song, ramping up in speed. Willie found himself gripping his knees. The singer wailed something about sticking his knife down someone's throat, and then, the song was over.

"The blues had a baby," Willie said, clapping furiously. The song danced on the razor's edge of good taste without apology, much as Willie had lived his life. He was struck with a sudden thought—B. B. King, a blues legend, playing on the same stage as white boys from England, like they all belonged together. All of them drinking from the same well—a well that ran so deep, the bottom rested in Africa.

Near the end of the concert, the Stones played one of their hits—*Satisfaction*—and the motionless girl sprang up in her seat like a jack-in-the-box, waving her arms and dancing spastically. The boy sitting next to her flinched as if she'd been resurrected, which in a way, she had. The usher who'd been standing in the aisle tried to dance, too. Thin and gawky, he tripped himself and plummeted down the steps. Several rows down, he stood and began dancing again.

When the concert finished, Willie let others head for the aisles first rather than risk his joints to the jostling crowd. He sat quietly, smelling the odd, sweet smoke around him, relishing the secondhand high. Watching popular bands play was not something he'd do again any time soon—too hard on his old body—but he'd enjoyed himself. Everything new and wonderful, and somehow rooted in his own past.

When the aisles were clear, he left his seat and started the walk home. He took his time. The walk was short, and the night was crisp with cold. If he kept moving at a slow, steady pace, his hip would let him be. He noticed an odd, satisfied sort of feeling that warmed him in the cold night air, and tried to identify it. Seeing a bluesman celebrated as a legend was gratifying. Listening to the Stones and their dirty sound was nice, too. A new generation, taking the music somewhere new.

Leaving campus, he stepped off the curb wrong and felt something pop. His hip screamed in protest. To take his mind off the pain, he began talking to himself. "Kennedy would have liked that show. Wish he'd been here tonight." In his life, Willie had cared for just a handful of people. Jackwash—his oldest, dearest friend. Luella—the only woman he'd ever loved. And Kennedy. Thinking of the boy's letter, Willie laughed. Underage drinking and girl troubles? History repeats itself.

That was what the night had been about. The concert had given him a sense of history. *His* history. The people in the seats couldn't tell him apart from the Maytag repairman, but better than any of them, he understood the context of the music. He'd loved the blues as much as any person there, and though the music hadn't always loved him back, he'd played his part. Now, half the world was listening.

Almost home, he turned onto his street. A single lamppost cast shadows from leafless trees, like long fingers swallowed by the darkness. November clouds blanketed a starless sky. Ahead, his house sat like a dark spot at the end of a tunnel.

His hip throbbed and he ignored it, wondering instead what his friend Jackwash would have thought of all those cowtown kids, singing along to B.B. King. "Wouldn't have surprised you at all," Willie said. "You watched *this* white boy play the blues your whole life." On the other hand, Jackwash would surely have made fun of the way the vocalist for the Stones danced. No self-respecting bluesman would fling himself around like that.

What would Luella have thought? *Shit, I sing better than any of those fools*.

"Yes, you surely did," Willie whispered.

Reaching his front door, he paused for a tired moment to think of his guitar and his songs, long nights in boxcars and barns, playing in jukes, whiskey and gin, grits and bacon fat, and his friends, Jackwash and Luella. Then, with the flicker of a smile, like a candle in an upstairs window, he stepped inside.

AUTHOR'S NOTES

First, some words of thanks. Laura Mahal did a phenomenal job of editing the final draft of this book. The fact that she didn't have to tear her hair out in the process owes much to my two critique groups, *Raintree Writers* and the *Penpointers*.

Thanks also to Black Rose Writing. Reagan Rothe is a fearless publisher.

A historical novel is a blend of fact and fiction. Let me mention a few places where hard facts gave way to the necessities of storytelling.

I didn't have to do much research for the scenes set in Fort Collins, Colorado. My family moved to Colorado in August of 1969, and I crafted my settings from memory. Of course, memory is a foggy liar, so discrepancies surely exist.

Fort Collins was a dry town until 1969, allowing 3.2 beer within the city limits, but not liquor. Because the novel ends with the Rolling Stones concert in November of that year, I had a fixed timeline to deal with. I played fast and loose with some details to be able to mention some old Fort Collins businesses I frequented (and loved) back in the day. I also changed a name or two. More on that later.

The ancient "blues legend" character at the Spinning Mule juke who told my novel's protagonist that the blues are "not a race" was loosely (very loosely) based on Robert Curtis Smith, the pride of Cruger, Mississippi.

The historical Willie Johnson—Blind Willie Johnson—got a passing mention in my novel. Blind Willie was a blues singer turned preacher who died in 1945. He played a fine slide guitar. I'm partial to his song, *Dark was the Night; Cold was the Ground*. When NASA sent *Voyager* into space in 1977, that song was included on the twenty-seven-song gold record disk that was part of the space probe's payload.

I liked Willie's name (and if you've read the novel, you know why). I also liked the idea of an unknown playing at the periphery of blues history with a name he has to share. A lot of guys named Sonny, Lightning and Blind Boy would understand.

Now, a few words about underage drinking. In the 1960s, it was not uncommon to sell liquor to minors. The drinking age wasn't taken as seriously back then, and the idea that someone old enough to die in Viet Nam ought to be able to vote and drink may have affected how some businesses approached age restrictions. Growing up, I had no trouble purchasing alcohol underage outside of town. Nevertheless, several of the twelve bars mentioned in *Sins in Blue* have been fictionalized to avoid linking places I loved to my particular habits and attitudes.

The 1960s were a different world. Some changes are for the better.

The main theme of *Sins in Blue*—cultural appropriation—is an important contemporary issue, open to discussion. Like Willie, I think more of people's actions than I do of words (surprising, perhaps, coming from an author). In my view, a person committed to diversity is more likely to embrace aspects of other cultures and take them in rather than setting boundaries and acting as gatekeeper. The latter strikes me as the same old Jim Crow behaviors with a brand-new wrapper.

But starting a dialog was not my main purpose in writing the story. My primary motivation was to craft a love letter to my favorite music. My own blues journey began with the discovery of a four-song EP by harmonica virtuoso Sonny Terry in a record store bargain bin. I heard *Women's Blues (Corrina)* once and was hooked for life. I recently gave that EP away to a young friend who plays guitar like a house on fire. Important things should be handed down.

My second motivation for *Sins in Blue* was to write a tragic love story. Son House said that the blues was about love, and I agree.

Finally, I wanted, through Willie's story, to "play" a few songs that I'd written but could never perform. I can't sing a lick, and my guitar work is forever slow, cramped, and awful.

But Willie? That guy could *play*.

Brian Kaufman
Laporte, Colorado 2019

GLOSSARY

Abyssinia: "I'll be seeing you."
Box: Guitar
Bull: Railroad cop
Gig: A paying job for a musician
Gobble-pipe: Saxophone
Going dizzy: Falling in love
H: Heroin
Harp: Harmonica
Jeff: A generic name for someone who's "uncool"
Machine heads: Tuning knobs on a guitar
Mexican mud: Heroin from Mexico
Outro: The concluding piece of a musical composition
Sterno: Wax soaked with alcohol
T: Marijuana
Trip for biscuits: A worthless errand

QUOTE ATTRIBUTIONS

The song lyrics in "Sins in Blue" are the original work of the author. Some chapter headers, however, used actual quotes (listed below with sources for your reference):

"Young people have forgotten to cry the blues. Now they talk and get lawyers and things."
~Big Bill Broonzy
https://brainyquote.com/quotes/big_bill_broonzy_2650087?src+t_blues

"Saturday night is your big night. Everybody used to fry up fish and have one hell of a time. Find me playing till sunrise for 50 cents and a sandwich. And be glad of it."
~Muddy Waters
 https://brainyquote.com/quotes/muddy_waters_196670

"Ain't but one kind of blues, and that consists between a male and female that's in love…"
~Son House https://quotefancy.com/quote/1758465/Son-House-Aint-but-one-kind-of-blues-and-that-consists-of-a-male-and-female-that-s-in

"It's easier for a camel to pass through the eye of a needle than for a rich man to make a blues record."
~Hugh Laurie
 https://brainyquote.com/quotes/hugh_laurie_593182?src=t_blues

"Some of the greatest blues music is some of the darkest music you've ever heard."
~Bruce Springsteen

https://brainyquote.com/quotes/bruce_springsteen_460844?scr=t_blues

"Audiences like their blues singers to be miserable."
~Janis Joplin
 https://brainyquote.com/quotes/janis_joplin_379275?scr=t_blues

ABOUT THE AUTHOR

Brian Kaufman is curriculum editor for an online junior college. His published writing includes six novels, three textbooks and three novellas. In other universes, he is a pro wrestler, a radio talk show host or center fielder for the Yankees. In this universe, he lives with his wife and dog in the Colorado Mountains, avoiding moderation and any pretense of maturity.

NOTE FROM THE AUTHOR

Word-of-mouth is crucial for any author to succeed. If you enjoyed *Sins in Blue*, please leave a review online—anywhere you are able. Even if it's just a sentence or two. It would make all the difference and would be very much appreciated.

    Thanks!
    Brian

Thank you so much for reading one of our **Literary Fiction** novels.

If you enjoyed our book, please check out our recommended title for your next great read!

The Five Wishes of Mr. Murray McBride by Joe Siple

2018 Maxy Award "Book of the Year"

"A sweet...tale of human connection...will feel familiar to fans of Hallmark movies." –*KIRKUS REVIEWS*

"An emotional story that will leave readers meditating on the life-saving magic of kindness." –*Indie Reader*

View other Black Rose Writing titles at www.blackrosewriting.com/books and use promo code **PRINT** to receive a **20% discount** when purchasing.

Lightning Source UK Ltd.
Milton Keynes UK
UKHW011838200520
363522UK00001B/26